D1381234

Happy Are the Happy

YASMINA REZA is a French playwright and novelist, based in Paris. Both her novels and plays have been translated worldwide. Her plays are multi-award-winning critical and popular international successes; *Conversations After a Burial*, *'Art'*, *The Unexpected Man*, *Life x 3*, *A Spanish Play* and *God of Carnage* have been translated into thirty-five languages and produced all over the world. *God of Carnage* was made into the film *Carnage*, directed by Roman Polanski, and *A Spanish Play* inspired the film *Chicas*, which was directed by Yasmina Reza herself. Her novels include *Hammerklavier*, *Desolation*, *Adam Haberberg* and *Dawn, Dusk or Night*.

SARAH ARDIZZONE was born in Brussels and lives in Brixton. She has translated some forty titles from the French, winning the Scott Moncrieff Prize, the Marsh Award for Children's Literature in Translation and a New York Times Notable Book accolade. Like Yasmina Reza, Sarah originally trained in theatre with Jacques Lecoq in Paris.

Also by Yasmina Reza
in English translation

Novels
Hammerklavier
Desolation
Adam Haberberg
Dawn, Dusk or Night

Plays
Conversations After a Burial
'Art'
The Unexpected Man
Life x 3
God of Carnage

Screenplays
Lulu Kreutz's Picnic

Yasmina Reza

Happy Are the Happy

Translated from the French by
Sarah Ardizzone

Harvill Secker
London

Published by Harvill Secker 2014

2 4 6 8 10 9 7 5 3 1

First published with the title *Heureux les heureux* in 2013 by Flammarion, Paris

First published in Great Britain in 2014 by
Harvill Secker
Random House
20 Vauxhall Bridge Road
London SW1V 2SA

www.vintage-books.co.uk

Addresses for companies within The Random House Group Limited
can be found at: www.randomhouse.co.uk/offices

The Random House Group Limited Reg. No. 954009

A CIP catalogue record for this book is available from the British Library

ISBN 9781846558009 (hardback)
ISBN 9781448182725 (ebook)

This book is supported by the Institut Français (Royaume-Uni)
as part of the Burgess programme (www.frenchbooknews.com)

INSTITUT
FRANÇAIS

Designed in Times and Optima by Andrew Woodhead
Typeset by Palimpsest Book Production Limited.
Printed and bound in Great Britain by Clays Ltd, St Ives Plc

To Moïra

'Felices los amados y los amantes y los que
pueden prescindir del amor. Felices los felices.'

'Happy are the loved and the lovers and those
who can do without love. Happy are the happy.'

Jorge Luis Borges

Robert Toscano

We were doing the weekend shop at the supermarket. At one point she said, you go and queue for the cheese while I deal with the groceries. When I came back, the trolley was half full of cereals, biscuits, powdered food sachets and creamy desserts. I said, what's the point in any of that? – What d'you mean, what's the point? I said, where's the sense in any of that? – You've got children, Robert, they like Cruesli, they like Napolitains, and they have a soft spot for Kinder Bueno; she was holding up the packets for me. I said, it's ludicrous to stuff them full of fat and sugar, this trolley is ludicrous, and she said, which cheeses did you buy? – A Chavignol and some Morbier. She shrieked, and

1

no Gruyère? – I forgot and I'm not going back, it's too busy. – If you're only buying one cheese, you know perfectly well it has to be Gruyère, who eats Morbier at home? Who? Me, I said. – Since when do you eat Morbier? Who wants to eat Morbier? I said, stop it, Odile. – Who likes bloody Morbier?! Meaning: 'apart from your mother'. Recently, my mother had found a rivet in a Morbier. I said, you're shouting, Odile. She manhandled the trolley and tossed in a three-pack of Milka bars. I fished out the bars and put them back on the shelf. In a flash, she put them back in the trolley. I said, I'm off. She replied, off you go then, off you go, all you ever say is I'm off, it's your stock response, as soon as you're running low on excuses you say I'm off, out comes this preposterous threat. She's right, I often say I'm off, I admit I say it, but I don't see how I could not say it, when it's the only urge I have, when I can see no way out apart from instant desertion, but I also admit, yes, that I use it as an ultimatum. Right, have you finished your shopping, I say to Odile, giving the trolley a shove forward, we don't have any other crap to buy? – Listen to how you're talking to me! Do you have any idea how you're talking to me? I say, keep moving. Keep moving! Nothing irritates me more than these sudden instances of piqued pride, when everything stops, when everything is transfixed. Of course I could say, I'm sorry. Not once, I'd have to say it twice, in the right tone of voice. If I said I'm sorry, twice, in the right tone of voice, we could almost carry on normally with our day, except that I have no urge, no physiological possibility of saying such words when she stops in the middle of a row of condiments, as if stunned by insult and calamity. Keep moving please, Odile, I say in a controlled voice, I'm hot and I have an article to finish. Apologise, she says. If she'd said apologise in a normal tone, I might have backed down, but she murmurs, she makes her voice deliberately flat, atonal, and there's no way round that. I say, please, and I keep calm, please, in a controlled voice, I picture myself speeding round a ring road, listening at full blast to 'Sodade', a song I've recently discovered, and which I don't understand at all, apart from the loneliness of the voice, and the word solitude repeated over and over again, even if people tell me the word doesn't mean solitude but nostalgia, loss, regret, melancholy, a host of intimate things that cannot be shared but which are known as solitude, just as the domestic trolley, the aisle of oils and vinegars, and the man begging his wife under the fluorescent lighting are known as solitude. I say, I'm sorry. I'm sorry, Odile. Odile is an unnecessary addition. Of course it is. Odile isn't nice. I say *Odile* as a sign of my impatience, but I'm not expecting her to turn, arms dangling, towards the refrigerated-goods section, at the back of the shop, without a word, leaving her handbag in the trolley. What are you doing, Odile? I shout, I've got two hours left to write a major piece on the new gold rush! I sound completely ridiculous. She's disappeared from sight. People are staring at me. I grab the trolley and make a dash for the back of the shop, I can't see her (she's always had a talent for disappearing, even in happier circumstances). I shout, Odile! I head towards the drinks: nobody. Odile! Odile! I sense I'm alarming the people around me, not that I care, I plough up and down the aisles with the trolley, God I hate supermarkets, and all of a sudden I spot her, in the cheese queue, a queue that's even longer than it was a moment ago, she's gone back to join the cheese queue! Odile, I say, once I'm level with her, I'm speaking in a measured voice, Odile, you'll have to wait twenty minutes to be served, let's go and we'll buy the Gruyère somewhere else. No reply. What does she do? She rummages in the trolley and picks up the Morbier. I say, you're not going

4

to return the Morbier? – Yes. We'll give it to Mum, I say to lighten the mood. Recently, my mother found a screw in some Morbier. Odile doesn't smile. She stands there, the upright injured party in the line of penitents. My mother told the cheesemonger, I don't like to make a fuss but, given your reputation as a purveyor of fine cheeses, I should point out that I found a metal rivet in your Morbier. The guy didn't give a damn, he didn't even offer her the three Rocamadours she was buying that day as a goodwill gesture. My mother prides herself on having paid without batting an eyelid and of being bigger than the cheesemonger. I walk up to Odile and I say, quietly, I'm going to count to three, Odile. I'm going to count to three. Do you hear me? Now why, just as I say that, do I think of the Hutners, a couple we're friends with, who have withdrawn into a show of smug-marriedness, they've started addressing each other, of late, as 'my heart', and they say things like 'let's cook something special this evening, my heart'. I don't know why the Hutners spring to mind when I'm possessed by the opposite kind of lunacy, but perhaps there isn't such a big divide between let's cook something special this evening, my heart and I'm going to count to three, Odile, in both cases there's a sort of constraining of the self in order to become two, by which I mean there's no more natural harmony in let's cook something special, my heart, oh no, and no less of a gulf either, except that I'm going to count to three has prompted a twitch in Odile's face, a puckering of her mouth, the tiny beginnings of a laugh, to which of course I simply mustn't succumb for as long as I don't have a clear green light, however strong the urge, no I've got to pretend I haven't seen a thing. I decide to count, I say *one*; I whisper it clearly, the woman just behind Odile has a ringside seat, with the toe of her shoe Odile pushes away some wrapping that's trailing on the floor, the queue is getting longer and it's not moving at all, I need to say two, I say *two*, it's an open two, magnanimous, the woman behind glues herself to us, she's wearing a hat, a sort of upturned floppy felt bucket, I can't bear women who wear hats like that, the hat is a very bad sign, my glare is intended to make her back off by a metre but nothing happens, she stares at me curiously, she looks me up and down, does she smell atrociously bad? There's often an odour that emanates from women who wear outfits that are stacked, unless it's the proximity of fermented dairy products. Inside my jacket, my mobile vibrates. I squint to read the caller's name because I don't have time to find my glasses. It's a contributor who might be able to tip me off about the Bundesbank's gold reserves. I ask him to send me an email because I'm in a meeting, which is what I say as shorthand. This could be a lucky phone call: I lean over and whisper into Odile's ear, in a voice that has resumed its responsibilities, my editor wants a focus piece on the state secret of Germany's stockpiling, and I haven't got anything on it yet. She says, who's interested in that? And she puckers her face, curling down the corners of her mouth so that I can see how inane the topic is, but more seriously still how inane my work is, and my efforts in general, as if there was no more hope for me, not even a recognition of my own sacrifices. Women take every opportunity to dump you in it, they love to remind you how disappointing you are. Odile has just moved up a place in the cheese queue. She has picked up her handbag and is still gripping the Morbier. I'm hot. I'm suffocating. I'd like to be far away, I don't know what we're doing here any more or what any of this is about. I'd like to slide on snowshoes in Western Canada, like Graham Boer, the gold digger and hero of my article, to plant stakes and mark the trees with an axe in frozen valleys. Does he have a wife and children, this Boer? A guy who braves grizzly bears and temperatures of minus thirty wouldn't have any truck with supermarket shopping at peak time. Is this a man's place? Who can walk down these aisles of fluorescent lighting, past never-ending packs, without feeling demoralised? And to think I'll be back, come rain or shine, whether I want to or not, dragging the same trolley under the orders of a woman who's becoming increasingly set in her ways. Not long ago, my father-in-law, Ernest Blot, said to our nine-year-old son, I'm going to buy you a new pen, you're staining your fingers with that one. Antoine replied, it's not worth it, I don't need to be happy with a pen any more. That's the secret, said Ernest, the child has understood: reduce the demand for happiness to a minimum. My father-in-law is the champion of fanciful maxims, which are worlds apart from his own temperament. Ernest has never made the slightest concession to anything that might reduce his vital potential (forget about the word happiness). Forced to observe the rhythm of the convalescent after his coronary bypass operations, and faced with a modest re-apprenticeship to life and the domestic servitude he'd always dodged, he felt singled out and struck down by God himself. Odile, if I say three, if the number three escapes my lips, you won't see me any more, I'll take the car and I'll leave you stranded here with the trolley. She says, I'd be surprised. – Surprised you may be, but that's what I'm going to do in two seconds time. – You can't take the car, Robert, the keys are in my bag. I rummage in my pockets like a fool because I can remember handing over the keys. Give them back, please. Odile smiles. She wedges her bag, which is slung across her shoulder, between her body and the front of the cheese counter. I step forward to tug at the bag. I tug. Odile resists. I tug at the strap. She hangs on to it and pulls in the other direction. She thinks it's funny! I grab hold of the bottom of the bag, I'd have no difficulty wrenching it off her in any other situation. She laughs. She tightens her grip. She says, aren't you going to say three? Why don't you say *three*? She's getting on my nerves. And the keys in the bag, they're getting on my nerves too. But I love it when Odile is like this. And I love seeing her laugh. I'm just about to relax into a mischievous game when I hear a snigger right up close to us, and I see the woman with the felt hat, drunk on female complicity, burst out laughing, brazenly. So I have no choice. I turn savage. I pin Odile against the Plexiglas and try to find a way into the opening of the bag, she struggles, complains that I'm hurting her, I say, give me those fucking keys, she says, you're crazy. I grab the Morbier out of her hands, I chuck it into the aisle, at last I can feel the keys in the jumble of her bag, I dig them out, I jangle them before her eyes without relaxing my hold on her, I say, we're getting the hell out of here right now. The woman with the hat is looking terror-stricken, I say to her, you're not laughing any more, how come? I tug on Odile and the trolley, I lead them past the shelves, towards the exit tills, I grip her wrist tightly even though she's not putting up a fight, it's far from innocent, this kind of submissiveness, I'd rather be forced to drag her, I always pay for it in the end when she slips on her martyr costume. There's a queue at the tills of course. We take our place in this deadly wait-in-line, without exchanging a word. I've let go of Odile's arm and she poses as a normal customer, I can even see her sorting the items in the trolley and establishing a little order to help with the bagging-up. In the car park, we don't say anything. The same in the car. It's dark. The lights from the road make us drowsy and I put on the CD of the Portuguese song with the woman's voice repeating the same word over and over again.

Marguerite Blot

In the distant era of my marriage, in the hotel where we used to spend our summers *en famille*, there was a woman we would see every year. Cheerful, elegant, grey hair in a sporty cut. Always present, she moved from group to group and dined each night at a different table. Often, in the late afternoons, she was to be seen sitting with a book. She chose a corner of the lounge from where she could keep an eye on the comings and goings. The moment she saw somebody she recognised, her face would light up and she would flutter her book like a handkerchief. One day she arrived with a tall brunette in a diaphanous pleated skirt. They were inseparable. They lunched in front of the lake, played tennis, played cards. I enquired who the brunette was and I was told a lady's companion. I accepted the term as you do an ordinary term, a term without any particular meaning. Every year at the same time, they appeared and I would think to myself, there goes Madame Compain and her lady's companion. Next came a dog, held on a lead by one or the other, although it clearly belonged to Madame Compain. All three of them could be seen setting out in the morning, the dog dragging them along, as they tried to keep it in check by calling out its name in every tone imaginable, but to no avail. In February, this winter, and therefore many years later, I headed for the mountains with my son, who is all grown up now. He goes skiing of course, with his friends, and I walk. I enjoy walking, I enjoy the forest and the silence. At our hotel, some walks were pointed out to me, but I didn't undertake any of them because of the distance. One can't be alone and too far away in the mountains and the snow. I chuckled at the thought of putting up a notice at reception: single woman seeks pleasant person to go walking with. Madame Compain and her lady's companion immediately sprang to mind, and I realised what *lady's companion* meant. I was frightened that I misunderstood, because Madame Compain had always struck me as a woman who was somewhat lost. Even when she was laughing with people. Perhaps especially, now I come to think about it, when she was laughing and dressed up for the evening. I turned towards my father, by which I mean I raised my eyes to the sky and whispered, Daddy, I can't become a Madame Compain! It had been a long time since I had addressed my father. Since his death, I ask him to intervene in my life. I stare at the sky and speak to him secretly but vehemently. He's the only being I can turn to when I feel powerless. Other than him, I don't know anybody who would take any notice of me in the beyond. It never occurs to me to talk to God. I've always maintained you can't bother God. You can't talk to him directly. He hasn't got time to take an interest in individual cases. Or at least only in exceptionally serious cases. In the scale of entreaties, mine are, so to speak, ridiculous. I feel much the same as my friend Pauline did when she found her necklace, inherited from her mother, lost in the long grass. As they were passing through a village, her husband stopped the car to rush into the church. The door was locked, he started rattling the latch frantically. – What on earth are you doing?

I want to give thanks to God, he replied. – God doesn't give a hoot! – I want to give thanks to the Holy Virgin. – Listen, Hervé, if there is a God, if there is a Holy Virgin, do you really think that in the light of the universe, and all the misfortunes on earth, and everything else that's going on here, my necklace matters to them?! . . . So I call upon my father who seems more within reach. The favours I ask of him are clearly defined. Perhaps because circumstances are such that I require something specific, but also, in a subterranean kind of way, to gauge what he's capable of. It's always the same call for help. A petition for something to shift. But my father is useless. He can't hear me or else he has no power. It's pathetic that the dead should be powerless. I disapprove of this radical division of worlds. From time to time, I credit him with prophetic knowledge. I think: he's not granting your requests because he knows they're not in your best interests. You're getting on my nerves, I feel like saying, what are you meddling for, but at least that way I can consider his non-intervention as deliberate. That's what he did with Jean-Gabriel Vigarello, the last man I fell for. Jean-Gabriel Vigarello is a colleague, a mathematics teacher at the Lycée Camille-Saint-Saëns, where I teach Spanish. With hindsight, I tell myself that my father wasn't wrong. But what is hindsight? It's old age. My father's celestial values exasperate me, they're terribly bourgeois when you think about it. In his lifetime, he believed in the stars, in haunted houses and in all sorts of esoteric knick-knackery. My brother Ernest, who has turned his lack of belief into a justification for vanity, resembles him a little more each day. Recently, I heard Ernest repeating of his own volition: 'the stars influence but don't dictate'. My father was crazy about that maxim, which I'd forgotten, and he would add the name of Ptolemy in a half-threatening manner. If the stars don't dictate, I thought, what would you know about the *immanent* future, Daddy? I became interested in Jean-Gabriel Vigarello the day I noticed his eyes. It wasn't easy to notice them, given his haircut: long hair, obliterating his forehead, a haircut that was at once ugly and impossible for somebody of his age. My first thought was, this man has a wife who doesn't look after him (he's married, of course). You don't let a man of nearly sixty go about with a haircut like that. And, more importantly, you say to him: don't hide your eyes. Changeable blue-grey eyes, that shimmer like lakes at

15

altitude. One evening, I ended up alone with him in a café in Madrid (we had organised a trip to Madrid with three classes), and I was bold enough to say, you have the sweetest eyes, Jean-Gabriel, it's madness to try and hide them, really it is. One thing led to another. After that line and a bottle of Carta de Oro, we wound up in my hotel room, which overlooked a courtyard complete with meowing cats. On our return to Rouen, he immediately threw himself back into his normal life. We bumped into one another in the school corridors as if nothing had happened, he always seemed to be in a rush, his briefcase in his left hand and his body leaning to the same side, his greying fringe obscuring more than ever. I find it shoddy, this habit men have of banishing us out of time. As if we needed reminding, for our information, that life is intermittent. I thought, I'll leave a note in his pigeonhole. An inconsequential word or two, witty, including a Madrid detail. I left the note, one morning when I knew he was there. No answer. Not that day, nor in the days that followed. We greeted each other as if nothing had gone on. I fell victim to a sort of despondency, I wouldn't call it despondency in love, no, but rather despondency at being abandoned. There's a poem by

Borges which begins with: '*Ya no es mágico el mundo. Te han dejado.*' 'And the world is no longer magical. They have left you.' He says *left,* an everyday word, which makes no noise. Anybody can leave you, even a Jean-Gabriel Vigarello with his Beatles haircut fifty years on. I asked my father to intervene. In the meantime, I had written another note, a single phrase: 'Don't blot me out completely. Marguerite.' I thought the word blot was ideal to dispel his fears, if he had any. A gentle reminder expressed as banter. I said to my father, I cut a cheerful figure but as you can see nothing's happening and soon I'll be old. I said to my father, I'll be leaving the lycée at five o'clock, it's nine o'clock now, you've got eight hours to inspire Jean-Gabriel Vigarello's reply which I'll find in my pigeonhole or on my mobile. My father didn't lift a finger. With hindsight, I'll concede he was right. He has never approved of my absurd infatuations. He's right. You pluck a face from the crowd, you invent a beacon in time. Everybody wants a story to tell. In the past, I would leap into the future without thinking twice. Madame Compain was doubtless the sort to indulge in absurd infatuations. When she used to arrive alone at the hotel, she brought several suitcases with her. Every evening, we would see her in a different dress, a different necklace. She wore so much lipstick it rubbed off on her teeth, which contributed to her elegance. She moved from one table to another, had a glass or two with one group and then another, she was very lively, striking up conversation, particularly with the men. At the time I was with my husband and my children. A little unit, in the warm, from which one looks out on the world. Madame Compain flitted about like a moth. In any corner where the light filtered through, however feebly, Madame Compain would pop up with her lace wings. Since childhood, I've drawn time diagrams in my head. I see the year as an isosceles trapezium. Winter is at the top, a straight and confident line. Autumn and spring are pinned down as the sides of the skirt. And summer has always been a long flat floor. Today, it looks to me as if the angles have gone slack, the shape is no longer stable. What is this a sign of? I can't become a Madame Compain. I'm going to give my father a serious talking-to. I'm going to tell him that he has a unique opportunity to reveal himself for my benefit. I'm going to ask him to get the geometry of my life back in shape. It's something very simple and easy to bring about. Could you, I'm planning to ask him, send somebody cheerful my way, somebody I could laugh with and who would enjoy walking? You must know somebody who would wear his scarf with the ends nice and flat, crossed over inside an old-fashioned coat, somebody who would hold me with a strong arm and take me off without us getting lost in the snow and the woods.

Odile Toscano

Everything bugs him. Opinions, things, people. Everything. We can't go out these days without it ending badly. Bottom line, it's me who ends up persuading him to come along, and I nearly always regret it. We take our leave with a few idiotic niceties, we laugh out on the landing, and in the lift the chill kicks in. One day somebody should study this silence, which is particular to the car, at night, when you're on the way home, after making a public display of contentment for the gallery, blending indoctrination with self-deception. It's a silence that won't even tolerate the radio, since who, in this wordless war, would dare to switch it on? Tonight, as I'm getting undressed, Robert, as usual,

21

lingers in the children's bedroom. I know what he's doing. He's checking their breathing. He leans over and takes his time to make sure they're not dead. Next, we're in the bathroom, both of us. No communication. He's brushing his teeth, I'm taking off my make-up. He heads to the toilet. I find him sitting on our bed; he checks his emails on his BlackBerry, he sets his alarm. Then he worms his way between the sheets and immediately turns out the light on his side. I sit down on the opposite side of the bed, I set my alarm, I rub cream into my hands, I swallow a Stilnox, I put my earplugs within reach on the bedside table, alongside a glass of water. I arrange the cushions, I put on my glasses and settle down comfortably to read. I've scarcely begun when Robert, in a supposedly neutral tone of voice, says, turn it out, please. These are the first words to pass his mouth since we were on Rémi Grobe's landing. I don't answer. After a few seconds, he sits up and lies half across me to turn out my bedside light. He manages to turn it out. In the dark I hit him on the arm, on the back, I hit him several times, and I switch the light back on. Robert says, I haven't slept for three nights now, do you want me to croak? I don't look up from my book but I say, take a

Stilnox. – I don't take that kind of shit. – Well, don't complain then. – I'm tired, Odile . . . Turn out the light. Turn it out, for fuck's sake. He curls up under the sheets. I try to read. I wonder if the word *tired* in Robert's mouth hasn't contributed more to distancing us than anything else. I refuse to credit it with some existential meaning. You can accept a literary hero withdrawing into the realm of darkness, but not a husband with whom you share a domestic life. Robert switches his light back on, extricates himself from the sheets with an abruptness that is out of all proportion and sits on the edge of the bed. Without turning around he says, I'm going to a hotel. I say nothing. He doesn't move. I read for the seventh time: 'By the light still filtering through the battered shutters, Gaylor saw the dog lying under the commode, with its basin of chipped enamel. On the opposite wall, a man was staring sadly at him. Gaylor went over to the mirror . . .' Who's Gaylor again? Robert is hunched forward, with his back to me. From this position he intones, what have I done, did I talk too much? Am I aggressive? Do I drink too much? Have I got a double chin? Go on, reel off your list. What was it tonight? You talk too much, that's for sure, I say. – It was so bloody boring. And quite revolting. – Not very tasty, I agree. – Revolting. What the hell does he do in life, Rémi Grobe? – He's a consultant. – A consultant! What bright spark coined that word? I don't know why we inflict these ridiculous dinners on ourselves. – Nobody makes you come. – Yes they do. – No they don't. – Of course they do. And that silly bitch in red, who doesn't even know the Japanese haven't got the bomb! – What difference does it make? Who needs to know? – When somebody doesn't have any idea about Japanese defence strengths (and who does, by the way?) they shouldn't get mixed up in a conversation about territorial claims in the China Sea. I'm cold. I try to tug the duvet. By sitting on the side of the bed, Robert has inadvertently jammed it. I tug, he lets me tug but doesn't budge at all. I tug and I let out a little moan. This wordless struggle is completely idiotic. In the end he stands up and walks out of our bedroom. I turn back a page to find out who Gaylor is. Robert reappears quite quickly, he's put his trousers on. He looks for his socks, finds them, puts them on. He disappears again. I can hear him ferreting about in the corridor and opening a cupboard. Then it sounds like he returns to the bathroom. On the previous page, Gaylor is having an argument at the back of a garage with a man called Pal. Who is Pal? I get out of bed. I put on my slippers and join Robert in the bathroom. He has pulled on a shirt, without buttoning it up, and is sitting on the side of the bath. I ask, where are you going? He gives the wave of a man in despair, as if to say I don't know, anywhere. I say, d'you want me to make you up a bed in the sitting room? – Don't fuss about me, Odile, go to bed. – Robert, I've got four hearings this week. – Leave me alone, please. I say, come back, I'll turn the light out. I catch sight of myself in the mirror, Robert has turned on the bad light. I never use the ceiling light in the bathroom, or else only teamed with the basin spotlights. I say, I'm ugly. She cut my hair too short. Robert says, much too short. That's Robert's brand of humour. Half teasing, half alarming. He does it to make me laugh, even in the worst moments. But he also does it to alarm me. I say, are you serious? Robert says, what's he a consultant in, that fool? – Who are you talking about? – Rémi Grobe. – In art, in property, I don't know exactly. – A dabbler. So the guy's a crook. He's not married? – Divorced. – D'you find him good-looking? Out in the corridor, we hear a shuffling noise and a little voice: Mummy? What's his problem? asks Robert, as if I knew, and there's that instant note of alarm in his voice which makes me tense. I'm here, Antoine, I say, with Daddy in the bathroom. Antoine appears in pyjamas, half in tears. – I've lost Doodles. – Again! Are you going to lose Doodles every night now? At two o'clock in the morning, we don't worry about Doodles, it's sleepy time, Antoine! Antoine's face puckers almost in slow motion. When his face puckers like that, it's impossible to curb his tears. Robert says, why are you telling him off, poor kid? I'm not telling him off, I say, summoning all my powers of self-restraint, but I don't understand why we don't tie Doodles up. All we have to do is tie her up at night! I'm not telling you off, sweetheart, but now is not the time to worry about Doodles. Come on, back to bed. We head back to the boys' bedroom. Antoine whimpering, Dooooodles, Robert and me in single file in the corridor. We go into the bedroom. Simon is asleep. I ask Antoine to calm down a little so as not to wake up his brother. Robert whispers, we'll find her, badger. Are you going to tie her up? sighs Antoine without making any effort to lower his voice. I'm not going to tie her up, badger, says Robert. I turn on the bedside light and say, why not?

We can tie her up so she's nice and comfy. She won't feel anything and you'll have a little bit of string you can tug . . . Antoine starts wailing like a siren. Few children are in possession of such an exasperating plaintive range. Shhhhhh! I say. What's going on? asks Simon. – You see! You've gone and woken your brother up now, well done! – What are you doing? We've lost Doodles, says Robert. Simon stares at us, eyes half closed, as if we're morons. He's right. I crouch down to search under the base of the bed. I run my hand in every direction because I can't see much. Robert rummages about in the duvet. With my head under the bed, I mutter, I can't understand why you don't sleep in the middle of the night! This is just not normal. When you're nine, you sleep. All of a sudden, I can feel her, caught between the slats and the mattress. I've got her, I've got her. She's here! She can be a right pain in the neck, your Doodles . . . ! Antoine presses his soft toy to his mouth. Come on, bed! Antoine clambers into bed. I give him a kiss. Simon wraps himself in his sheets and turns over, like somebody who has just witnessed a depressing scene. I turn out the light. I start pushing Robert out of the bedroom. But Robert stays there. He wants to compensate for their mother's curtness. He wants to restore harmony to the enchanted bedroom of childhood. I can see him leaning over Simon and kissing his neck. Then, in the shadowy half-light which I make as dark as possible by pushing the door to, he sits down on Antoine's bed, on the edge, tucks him in, nestles him into his duvet, wedges Doodles so she can't escape. I can hear him whispering affectionately, it wouldn't surprise me if he hasn't embarked on one of Maître Janvier's stories from the woods. In days of old, men set out to hunt lions and conquer lands. I wait on the threshold, flapping one half of the double door to signal my exasperation, although my marmoreal stance is eloquent enough. Robert finally stands up. We make our way along the corridor, in silence. Robert enters the bathroom, and I the bedroom. I get back into bed. I put my glasses on. 'Pal was sitting at his desk. His chubby hands on the dirty blotter. That morning, he informed Gaylor, Raoul Toni had gone into the garage . . .' Who is Raoul Toni? My eyes close. I wonder what Robert's doing in the bathroom. I hear a footstep. He's here. He's taken off his trousers. How many times in our life, the crazy threat of these dressings and undressings? I say, do you think it's normal that he's still got a transitional object at the age of nine? – Of course. I still had one at eighteen. I want to laugh but I don't show it. Robert takes off his socks and shirt. He turns out his bedside light and slides between the sheets. I think I've understood who Gaylor is. Gaylor is the guy who's been hired to track down Joss Kroll's daughter, and I'm wondering if we didn't see Raoul Toni at the tombola, back near the beginning . . . My eyes are closing again. This crime novel is rubbish. I take off my glasses, switch out the light. I turn towards the bedside table. I notice I haven't drawn the curtains properly so the daylight will come in too early. Too bad. I say, why does Antoine wake up in the middle of the night? Because he can't feel Doodles, Robert replies. We stay there for a moment, each on our own side of the bed, staring at opposite walls. Then I turn over, once more, and press myself against him. Robert places his hand on the small of my back and says, I should tie you up as well.

Vincent Zawada

While she's waiting for her radiotherapy session at the Tollere Leman clinic, my mother gives a running commentary on every patient in the waiting room and says, in a voice she makes little effort to restrain, wig, wig, not sure, not wig, not wig . . . Mum, Mum, not so loud, I say, everybody's listening. What are you saying? You're mumbling into your beard, I can't understand a word, says my mother. – Have you got your ears? – What? – Have you got your ears on? Why aren't you wearing it? – Because I have to take it off for the radiation. – Put it in for now, Mum. It doesn't do any good, says my mother. Seated close to her, a man gives me a sympathetic smile. He's holding a beret in Prince of Wales check, and his pale complexion matches his old-fashioned English suit. Anyway, says my mother rummaging in her bag, I didn't even bring it with me. Back to her round-up, she barely lowers her voice to declare, she won't last the month, that one, I'm not the oldest, mind you, which is reassuring . . . Mum, please, I say, look, there's a fun little quiz in *Le Figaro*. – Fine, if it keeps you happy. – Which vegetable, previously unknown in France, did Queen Catherine de Medici introduce to the court? Artichoke, broccoli or tomato? Artichoke, says my mother. – Artichoke, well done. What was Greta Garbo's first job when she was fourteen? Apprentice at a barber's, stand-in for Shirley Temple in *Little Miss Broadway*, or herring-scaler at the fish market in her hometown of Stockholm? Herring-scaler in Stockholm, says my mother. – Apprentice at a barber's. Oh, well, there you go, says my mother, mind you I'm silly, since when did a herring have scales?! Since for ever, if you don't mind my saying, interjects the man sitting nearby as I notice his grey tie with pink polka dots, the herring has always had scales. Really? says my mother, no, no, herrings don't have scales, they're like sardines. Sardines have also always had scales, says the man. Sardines have scales, that's news to me, says my mother, did you know that, Vincent? Just like anchovies and sprats, adds the man, at any rate, I can safely deduce you don't eat kosher! He laughs, including me in his attempt at familiarity. Despite his yellowed teeth and sparse greying hair, there's something stylish about him. I nod amiably. Luckily, says my mother, luckily I don't eat kosher, not that I've got any appetite left. Who is your doctor? asks the man, gently loosening his polka-dot tie, having shifted position to aid conversation. Doctor Chemla, says my mother. Philip Chemla, the best, you won't find better, he's been keeping me going for six years, says the man. And me for eight, says my mother, proud of being kept going for longer. Lungs as well? asks the man. Liver, replies my mother, breast first then liver. The man nods like somebody who knows the drill. But I'm atypical, you see, my mother continues, I don't do things like everybody else, each time Chemla says to me, Paulette (he calls me Paulette, I'm his pet), you're totally atypical (translation, you should have snuffed it long ago). My mother laughs heartily, the man too. I'm wondering if it isn't high time we got back to the quiz. You're right, he's terrific, gushes my mother, who's becoming unstoppable, and personally I find him very attractive. The first time I saw him I said, are you married, Doctor? Do you have children? No children. I said, would you like me to show you how it's done? I squeeze her hand, with its skin that's dry and ravaged by medication, and I say, Mum, listen. What, says my mother, it's the truth, he was captivated, he laughed like crazy, like I've rarely seen a cancer specialist laugh. The man nods. He says, he's a great man, Chemla, a real *mensch*. One day, I'll never forget it, he had this to say: when a person walks into my consulting room, they are doing me an honour. You know he's not forty? My mother couldn't care less. She's in full flow now, it's as if she hasn't heard anything. On Friday, she booms even more loudly, I said to him, Doctor Ayoun (he's my cardiologist) is a much better doctor than you are. Oh, I'd be surprised, he said. Well, he is, he immediately complimented me on my new hat, whereas you, Doctor, you haven't even noticed it. I need to stretch my legs. I stand up and say, Mum, I'm going to ask the secretary how long it is before your turn. My mother turns towards her new friend: he's going to smoke, my son is going outside to smoke a cigarette, that's what he means, tell him he's slowly killing himself at forty-three. Well, that way we can die together, Mum, I say, look on the positive side. Very funny, says my mother. The man with the polka-dot tie pinches his nostrils and takes a deep breath as if he's about to make a critical announcement. I cut them short to point out that I'm not going outside to smoke even though a nicotine fix would do me a power of good, but that I'm just going to see the secretary. When I get back I inform my mother that she'll be having her radiation in ten minutes' time but that Doctor Chemla isn't there yet. Ah, that's Chemla for you, fuzzy with the watch, he doesn't consider we might have another life, says the man, glad to get his voice heard again and hoping to keep his hand in. But my mother has already launched her counter-attack: I'm on best terms with the secretary, she always bumps me up to the top of the list, I call her Virginie, she's got a soft spot for me, adds my mother in a whisper, I say to her, be a poppet, give me the first appointment, Virginie, my dear, she enjoys that, it makes her feel special. Vincent darling, don't you think we should bring her some chocolates next time? Why not, I say. – What? You're mumbling into your beard. I say, that's a good idea. We could have got rid of the Vanille Kipferl from Roseline, says my mother, I haven't even opened the box. She has no idea how to make them, it's like eating sand. Poor Roseline, she's a jangling bunch of keys these days. She's been a different woman since her daughter disappeared in the tsunami, you know, hers is one of the twenty-five bodies that were never found, Roseline believes she's still alive, which gets on my nerves from time to time, I want to say to her yes, in all likelihood adopted by chimpanzees who've turned her into an amnesiac. I say, don't be mean, Mum. – I'm not being mean but one does have to be fatalistic as well, we know that the world is a vale of tears. The vale of tears, one of your father's expressions, do you remember? Yes, I remember, I reply. The man with the polka-dot tie seems to have turned his mind to darker thoughts. He is leaning forward, and I notice a crutch tucked in alongside his chair. It occurs to me that some part of his body is in pain and I reflect that other people in this waiting room in the basement of the Tollere Leman clinic must also secretly be in pain. The thing is, says my mother all of a sudden, leaning towards the man with a surprisingly serious expression, my husband was obsessed with Israel. The man sits up and readjusts the rear of his striped suit. The Jews are obsessed by Israel, not me, I'm not obsessed by Israel one little bit, but my husband was. I'm having a hard time following my mother's change of tack. Unless she's trying to make up for the herrings-don't-have-scales gaffe. Yes, perhaps she wishes to make it clear that her entire family is Jewish, herself included, despite her knowing nothing about the basic laws. Are you obsessed with Israel too? asks my mother. Naturally, replies the man. I approve of this terseness. Left to my own devices, I could write a thesis on what had gone unsaid in that response. But my mother has another way of apprehending things. When I met my husband, he had nothing, she says, his family had a tiny haberdashery on rue Réaumur, it was a rathole. At the end of his life, he was a wholesaler, he had three shops and an apartment block. He wanted to leave it all to Israel. – Mum, what's got into you? What are you saying! It's the truth, says my mother, without bothering to turn around, we were a very united family, very happy, the only black mark was Israel. One day I told him that the Jews didn't need a country, and he nearly hit me. On another occasion, when Vincent wanted to take a trip down the Nile, he threw him out. The man is on the brink of making

37

a remark, but he's not quick enough, by the time he's parted his colourless lips, my mother's already off again. Chemla wants to put me on new medication. My body won't tolerate the Xynophren any more. My hands are falling apart, as you can see. He wants me to start chemo on a drip again, which will make me lose my hair. That's not definite, Mum, I point out, Chemla said a one-in-two chance. A one-in-two chance means a two-in-two chance, says my mother, dismissing my assertion with a wave of her hand, but I don't want to die like at Auschwitz, I don't want a shaved head at the end. If I have that treatment, I can kiss goodbye to my hair. At my age, I haven't got time to see it grow back again. And I can kiss goodbye to my hats as well. My mother shakes her head and looks upset. Sitting bolt upright she talks without stopping, her neck strained like that of a pious young girl. I'm not under any illusions you know, she says. I'm only here chatting with you in this horrible room to please my son and Doctor Philip Chemla. I'm his pet, he enjoys continuing to treat me. Between us, this radiation doesn't do any good, none at all. It's supposed to make me see the way I used to but every day my sight gets worse. Don't be like that, Mum, I say, they told you the results won't be immediate. What are you saying says my mother, you're mumbling into your beard. The results aren't instantaneous, I repeat. Not instantaneous means not guaranteed, says my mother. The truth is that Chemla can't be sure of anything. He's feeling his way. I'm his guinea pig, fine, he needs them. I'm a fatalist. On his deathbed, my husband asked me if I was still an enemy of Israel, the homeland of the Jewish people. No, I replied, of course not. What do you say to a man who's not going to be there any more? You say what he wants to hear. It's strange to get hung up on idiotic values. In the final hour, when everything's about to disappear. The homeland, who needs a homeland? Even life, beyond a certain point, is an idiotic value. Even life, don't you think? says my mother with a sigh. The man reflects on this. He could answer, as my mother appears to have paused her babbling on an oddly meditative note. Just then a nurse calls for Monsieur Ehrenfried. The man picks up his crutch, his beret in Prince of Wales check and a Loden coat from the chair next to him. Still seated, he leans towards my mother and whispers: life perhaps, but not Israel. Then he wedges his arm on the crutch and gets up with difficulty. Duty calls, he says, bowing his head, Jean

Ehrenfried, it was a pleasure. One senses that every movement takes its toll but his face remains cheerful. The hat you're wearing today, he adds, is it the same one that earned you the compliments of the cardiologist? My mother puts her hand to her hat to check. No, no, this one is the lynx. Doctor Ayoun's one is a sort of Borsalino with a black velvet rose. Allow me to compliment you on today's hat, it has ennobled this waiting room, says the man. It's my little lynx hat, says my mother, quivering. I've had it for forty years, does it still suit me? To perfection, says Jean Ehrenfried, waving goodbye with a twirl of his beret. We watch him walk away and disappear behind the radiotherapy-room door. My mother thrusts her bruised hands into her bag. She fishes out a powder compact and a lipstick and says, he limps, poor man, I wonder if he hasn't fallen in love with me?

Pascaline Hutner

We didn't see it coming. We had no idea it might turn out this way. No. Not Lionel, not me. We feel cut off and helpless. Who can we talk to about it? We need to find a way of talking about it, but who can we confide in? We need to discuss it with people we can trust, people who are sympathetic, and who show no sign of finding it funny. We can't bear any hint of a joke on the subject, even though we're fully aware, Lionel and I, that were this not our own son, we might well laugh about it. And, frankly, we'd probably laugh in company too, given half a chance. But we haven't even told Odile and Robert. And we've always been friends with the Toscanos, even if it's not so easy maintaining a relationship between couples. A meaningful one, that is. At the end of the day, real intimacy only happens between two people. Perhaps if we'd tried seeing each other separately, just the women or just the men, or even mixing it up (if Robert and I could ever find anything to say to one another in private). The Toscanos make fun of us for being joined at the hip. They've developed this mocking attitude, which I find rather tedious. We can't say anything these days without them making us feel like a couple preserved in an asphyxiating smugness. The other day, I was rash enough to mention that I'd cooked some turbot en croûte (I'm taking cookery lessons, they're great fun). Turbot en croûte? gasped Odile, as if I'd spoken in a foreign language. – Yes, turbot with a fish-shaped crust. – For how many of you? The two of us, I said, Lionel and me, it was for the two of us. For the two of you, that's scary! said Odile. Why? asked my cousin Josiane who was with us. I might well cook turbot en croûte just for me. Just for you, yes, that's a whole different matter, added Robert, not to be outdone, turbot en croûte with a fish-shaped crust just for you, that's tragic. As a general rule, I pretend not to catch what he's saying, so as not to poison the atmosphere. Lionel's not bothered by it. When I talk to him about my misgivings, he says they're jealous, that people often react aggressively to the happiness of others. If we told them what's really going on, I don't see how they could be jealous. But it's because we appear to be the perfect family that it's so difficult to admit disaster. I can see people like the Toscanos having a field day. I'd better go back a bit. Our son, Jacob, who's just turned nineteen, has always liked the singer Céline Dion. I make a point of saying *always* because he's been infatuated with her since he was very young. So, one day, as a child, he hears Céline Dion's voice in somebody's car. And he's love-struck. We buy him the album, then the next one, he plasters his bedroom wall with posters and we start living with a little fan who is, I imagine, just like thousands of other fans all over the world. Soon, we're invited to concerts in his bedroom. Jacob dresses up as Céline in one of my slips and lip-syncs to her voice. I remember he used to create a hairdo using the tape from the cassettes we had back then, which he unspooled. I'm not sure Lionel really enjoyed the show, but it was terribly funny. Even then we had to endure Robert's taunting, as he congratulated us on being terrifically tolerant and open-minded. But it was terribly funny. Jacob grew up.

Little by little, it wasn't enough for him to sing like her, he started talking like her and giving pretend interviews in a Canadian accent. He played Céline, and he played her husband René too. It was hilarious. And we laughed. He had her off pat. We would ask him questions, I mean we would be speaking to Jacob and he would answer as Céline. It was terribly funny. I don't know what went wrong. How did we get from a childish crush to this . . . I don't know what word to use . . . this unhinging of the mind? Of the person? One evening, at supper, the three of us were in the kitchen, and Lionel told Jacob that he was tired of hearing him act the buffoon in a Québécois accent. I'd made salt pork with lentils. It's a dish my two men usually go crazy for, but there was something sad in the air that night. Rather like when there are just the two of you and the other person withdraws, and you have a premonition of being abandoned. Jacob pretended not to understand the word *buffoon*. His response to his father, in his Québécois accent, was that despite the fact he'd been living in France for some time, he was a Canadian woman, and had no intention of denying his roots. Lionel raised his voice, saying it was getting beyond a joke, and Jacob retorted that

44

he wasn't going to 'bicker' because he had to look after his vocal cords. Ever since that dreadful evening, we began to live with Céline Dion in the body of Jacob Hutner. We weren't called Mum and Dad any more, but Lionel and Pascaline. And we ceased to have any further relationship with our real son. To begin with, we thought it was just a phase: teenagers are prone to going off the rails a bit. But when Bogdana, our cleaner, told us that he had asked her, ever so politely, for a humidifier for his voice (she was on the verge of remarking on how modest he was for such a major star), I sensed that things were getting out of hand. Without telling Lionel, men can be too black-and-white about these things, I went to see a magnetic healer. I had heard about people being possessed by entities. The magnetic healer explained to me that Céline Dion was not an entity. And that therefore he wasn't in a position to detach her from Jacob. An entity is a restless spirit that attaches itself to a living person. He couldn't set free a boy who was inhabited by somebody who sings every night in Las Vegas. The magnetic healer advised me to see a psychiatrist. Well, the word *psychiatrist* stuck in my throat like a wad of cotton wool. It took me a while to broach the subject at home. Lionel was more level-headed. I could never have got through this ordeal without Lionel being such a rock. My husband. My heart. A man who is true to himself, but never over-assertive, and for whom the tortuous path holds no appeal . . . One day, Robert said of Lionel, he's a man in search of happiness, but a 'cubic' kind of happiness. We laughed at this barbed remark, and I even gave Robert a little slap. Still, at the end of the day, *cubic* is the word. Solid. Upstanding, from every angle. We managed to take Jacob to a psychiatrist by telling him we were going to see an ENT specialist. The psychiatrist recommended a stay in a clinic. I was shocked by how easy it was to manipulate our son. Jacob blithely crossed the threshold of the mental health clinic, convinced he was entering a recording studio. A kind of studio-hotel for superstars, so they didn't have to travel every morning. The first day, when I walked into the bare white room, it was all I could do not to throw myself at his feet and beg his forgiveness for such an act of betrayal. We told everybody that Jacob was doing an internship abroad. Everybody, including the Toscanos. The only person to share our secret is Bogdana. She still insists on baking him Serbian biscuits with walnuts and poppy seeds, which he doesn't touch because Jacob doesn't like the same things he used to. Physically, he still looks normal, he doesn't try to impersonate a woman. This is something much more profound than imitation. Lionel and I have ended up calling him Céline. Sometimes, between ourselves, we even say *she*. Doctor Igor Lorrain, his psychiatrist at the clinic, reports that he's only unhappy when he watches the news. He's obsessed by the arbitrary nature of his good fortune and privilege. The nurses are in two minds about taking his television away, because he weeps over everything on the evening news, even if it's a harvest battered by a hailstorm. The psychiatrist is also concerned about another aspect of his behaviour. Jacob goes down to the main entrance hall to sign autographs. He wraps several scarves around his neck so as not to catch a cold, you can't take any risks with a world tour, the doctor jokes (I'm not keen on him), and he positions himself in front of the revolving door, convinced that visitors to the clinic have travelled from far and wide to see him. That's where he was when we arrived yesterday afternoon. I could see him from the car, before we'd reached the car park. He was bending over a child, behind the revolving glass door, looking absurdly friendly, scribbling in a little notebook. Lionel understands my silences. Once he'd parked the car, he stared at the plane trees and said, is he down there again? I nodded and we hugged because we didn't know what to say. Doctor Lorrain tells us that Jacob calls him Humberto. We've explained that's probably because he thinks he's Humberto Gatica, his sound engineer, I mean Céline's sound engineer. It stands to reason in a way, given they both look like Steven Spielberg. In a similar vein, we've heard Jacob call the nurse from Martinique by the name Oprah (as in Oprah Winfrey) and she squirms as if it was a compliment. Today has been so difficult. First of all he said, in that accent I simply can't imitate, you don't look very happy right now, Lionel and Pascaline. I'm terribly sensitive when it comes to other people's feelings and it pains me to see you like this. Would you like me to sing something to help lift your spirits? We said no, he should rest his voice, he already had enough work on with all his recordings, but he insisted. He made us sit down side by side, just like we used to when he was little, Lionel on a stool, me in a leatherette armchair. And standing there in front of us, with a great sense of rhythm, he started singing

48

a song called 'Love Can Move Mountains'. At the end, we did what we used to do when he was little, we gave him a big round of applause. Lionel put his arm around me to give me strength. When we left that evening, we overheard voices in the corridor calling out to each other in a Canadian accent. Hey, David Foster, come and take a look at this! Is Humberto down yet? Ask Barbra . . . ! She should take a two-year break as well . . . ! We heard them laughing and we knew that the care staff were having fun at the expense of Céline and his entourage. Lionel couldn't take it. He stormed into the room where they were sniggering and declared in a desperately serious voice, which instantly sounded ridiculous even to me, I am the father of Jacob Hutner. Silence. Nobody knew what to say. And I said, come on, Lionel, it's not such a big deal. And the nurses started mumbling an apology. And I tugged at my husband's sleeve. We couldn't even find the lift, we felt so helpless, and taking the stairs instead, our footsteps echoed as we headed down. It was nearly dark outside, and raining slightly. I put my gloves on and Lionel strode off in the direction of the car park without waiting for me. I called out after him, wait for me, my heart. He turned around, his eyes scrunched up in the drizzle, and I thought how small his head looked with his thinning hair under the street light. I thought, life has to go on, Lionel must go back to the office, we must stay cheerful. In the car, I said I wanted to go to the Russian Canteen, to drink vodka and eat piroshki. And then I asked, who do you think Barbra is? Barbra Streisand, said Lionel. – Yes, but in the clinic? Do you think it's the ward manager with the long nose?

Paola Suares

I'm very sensitive to lights. Psychically, I mean. I wonder if everybody's sensitive to light in this way or whether I'm particularly susceptible. Outdoor light I can cope with. Gloomy weather I can cope with. The sky is for everybody. People go through the same fog. But interiors turn us in on ourselves. The light in enclosed spaces attacks me personally. It strikes objects and my soul. Certain lights rob me of all sense of the future. When I was a child, I ate in a kitchen looking out onto a dark courtyard. The lighting from the ceiling made everything look depressing and forgotten by the world. When we arrived, towards eight in the evening, in front of the hospital in the 10th arrondissement where Caroline had just given birth, I suggested to Luc that he come up with me, but he said he would rather wait in the car. He asked me whether I'd be long and I said, no, no, although I found his question uncalled for, not to say tactless. It was raining. The street was deserted. Likewise the lobby of the maternity wing. I knocked on the bedroom door. Joël opened it. Sitting on the bed, in a dressing gown, pale and happy, Caroline was holding a tiny little girl in her arms. I leaned over. She was pretty. Very delicate features, and really very pretty. I didn't find it hard to say so or to congratulate them. It was extremely hot in the room. I asked for a vase for the anemones I'd brought. Joël told me that flowers weren't allowed and that I should take them back with me. I took off my coat. Caroline gave the baby to her husband and slipped into bed. Joël cradled the little bundle and jiggled her gently as he sat down, all puffed up with fatherly pride, in a leatherette armchair. Caroline got out a Jacadi catalogue and showed me the travel cot. I made a note of the reference. On a Formica shelf, there were still some half-unwrapped presents and several bottles of antibacterial hand gel. I asked whether there was a resuscitation service on the premises because I was close to suffocating. Caroline said they couldn't open the window because of the little one but offered me some faded fruit jellies instead. A disposable baby's bottle and a crumpled swaddling blanket lay in the transparent cot. Beneath the strange light of the ceiling lamp, every scrap of fabric, the sheets, towels and bibs, looked yellow. Within this enclosed, indescribably drab world, a life was starting out. I stroked the sleeping little girl's forehead, I kissed Joël and Caroline. Before heading outside, I put the anemones, floppy from the heat, on a counter in the lobby. In the car, I told Luc that my friend's daughter was very pretty. What are we doing? he asked. Are we going to yours? But I said, no. Luc seemed surprised. I said, I feel like a change. Just like that he switched on the ignition and started up the car. I sensed that he was annoyed. – I'm fed up with the easy option of going to mine every time. Luc didn't reply. I shouldn't have let it come out like that. I regretted saying *the easy option*, but you can't get everything right. It was still raining. We drove without talking. He parked just before Bastille. We walked to a restaurant he knew but it was full. Luc tried arguing with them but there was nothing doing. We were already a long way from the car and we'd driven round and round looking for a parking spot. At one point, in the street, I said I was cold and Luc said in what I felt was a tetchy tone of voice, let's go there. – No, why there? – You're cold. We walked into a place I didn't like at all and Luc immediately accepted the table the *patron* was offering us. Just as we were sitting down he asked me if I was happy with it. The evening had already taken one turn for the worse, I didn't have the strength to say no. He sat down opposite me, elbows on the table, hands clasped and fidgeting. I was still cold and couldn't take off my coat or scarf. The waiter brought the menu. Luc feigned interest. He looked haggard under the dull neon. A message came through on his mobile from his youngest daughter, which he showed me. 'We r eating raklet!' His wife and children were on holiday in the mountains. I resented Luc for his lack of sensitivity; off the record, I find doting parenthood pathetic. But I managed a friendly smile. She's a lucky girl, I said. Yes, said Luc. An emphatic yes. No delicacy. I wasn't in the mood to protect myself from that tone of voice. I said, aren't you joining them? – Yes, on Friday. I thought, he can go to hell. There was precisely nothing I could eat on the menu. Nor on any

54

menu in the world for that matter and I said, I'm not hungry, I'd just like a glass of cognac. Luc said, I fancy breaded escalope with fries. I was attacked by melancholia in our miserable, so-called intimate booth. The waiter wiped the varnished wooden table, which wasn't properly clean even after he was done. I wonder whether men, without their acknowledging it, are also attacked in this way? I thought about the little girl experiencing her first hours of life, swaddled in that waxen room. A story came to mind, which I immediately told Luc in order to plug the gap. One evening, at a dinner, a psychiatrist, who is also a psychoanalyst, repeats the words of one of his patients who suffers from loneliness. This patient had said to him, when I'm at home, I'm scared of somebody coming and seeing how alone I am. The psychoanalyst adds, with a gentle snigger, the guy's on a loop. I also mentioned this detail to Luc. And Luc, ordering a glass of white wine, sniggered in much the same way as had Igor Lorrain, the psychoanalyst, in a way that was stupid, banal and objectionable. I should have walked out, ditching him in the ridiculous booth, but instead I said, I want to see where you live. Luc feigned astonishment, as if he wasn't sure he'd understood. I repeated, I want to go to your place, to see how you live. Luc looked at me as if I was becoming slightly interesting again and he said in a sort of sing-song voice, aha, my place you saucy devil . . . ? I nodded in a vaguely mischievous kind of a way, while hating myself for simpering, for failing to hold my own when faced with Luc. But I did still say, returning to the previous topic (my glass of cognac had just arrived), did you like the story about the patient? Did you understand it to be a perfect allegory for absence? Absence of what? said Luc. – Of the other. Yes, yes, of course, said Luc, pressing down on the mustard pot. Are you sure you don't want anything to eat? At least take some fries. I took a fry. I'm not used to cognac, nor any other spirit. My head spins at the first sip. Luc hadn't even thought of taking me to a hotel. He's got so used to coming round to my place that he had no other ideas up his sleeve. Men are so set in their ways. We're the ones who generate movement. We exhaust ourselves trying to liven up love. Since I met Luc Condamine, I'm forever bending over backwards. Some noisy young people, full of energy, were now in the booth behind ours. Luc asked me whether I'd seen the Toscanos recently. We met at the Toscanos. Luc is Robert's best friend. They work on the same newspaper but Luc is a special correspondent. I told him I've been getting home late and that I'm not seeing many people at the moment. Luc said that Robert seemed depressed and he'd introduced him to a girl. This surprised me because I've never taken Robert for the same kind of man as Luc. I said, I didn't know Robert had affairs. – He doesn't, which is why I'm looking out for him. I reminded him that as Odile's friend I couldn't share in such secrets. Luc laughed and wiped his mouth. He pinched my cheek half pityingly. He had already wolfed down his bowl of fries and was attacking the rest of his escalope. I said, who is it? – Oh no, Paola! You're Odile's friend, you don't want to know! – Who is it? Do I know her? – No, you're right, it'd be ugly if you found out. – Yes, very ugly. Spit it out. – Virginie. Medical secretary. – Where d'you know her from . . . ? With a sweep of his hand, Luc sketched his vast network of acquaintances. I was cheerful all of a sudden. I had drunk the entire glass of cognac with uncommon haste. But I was cheerful because so was Luc again. He ordered an apricot tart with two spoons. It was too acidic and creamy but we fought over the last piece of fruit. The young people were laughing behind us and I felt young like them. I said, are you taking me to your place, Luc? He said, let's go. I didn't know whether it was a good idea any more. My head wasn't too clear. For a short while, things still had a lightness about them, as we ran through the rain. In the car, at first, our mood remained light. Then I knocked one of the CDs from the central compartment. The disc fell out of its case and rolled under my seat. By the time I'd picked it up, Luc had already got hold of the case. Still driving, he took the CD from my hands and put it back in its container. Then he returned it to its initial position, tapping it so that everything was lined up again. All this took place without a sound. Without a word. I felt clumsy and perhaps even guilty of some indiscretion. I could have deduced from his overzealousness that Luc Condamine was obsessive, but stupidly I felt the urge to cry like a child caught in the act. I no longer thought it was a good idea to go to his place. In the foyer of his apartment block, Luc opened a glass door with his keys. Beyond, there was a pram and a folded buggy fastened to the banister. Luc ushered me in front of him and we climbed to the third floor, up a stairwell with an invisible lift bitten out of it. Luc switched on the lights in his apartment hallway. I could make out shelves lined with books and a coat rail with anoraks and coats hanging from it. I took mine off, together with my gloves and scarf. Luc showed me into the sitting room. He adjusted a halogen standard lamp and left me alone for a moment. There was a sofa, a coffee table, non-matching chairs, just like in every sitting room. An armchair in fairly worn leather. Shelves, books, photos in frames, including one of Luc, in the Oval Office, hypnotised by Bill Clinton. Miscellaneous objects. I sat down on the edge of the leather armchair. I had seen the print on the curtains somewhere before. Luc came back, he had removed his jacket. He said to me, do you want something to drink? I said, a cognac, as if in the space of one evening I had turned into a woman who drinks cognac as a matter of course. Luc brought over a bottle of cognac with two glasses. He sat down on the sofa and poured for us. He dimmed the lights, switched on a lamp with a pleated shade, and lolled back onto the cushions while eyeing me. I was perched on just a few centimetres of the armchair, upright, legs crossed, trying to look like Lauren Bacall with my drink. Luc sank further back into the sofa, legs splayed. Between him and me, on a sort of pedestal table, there was a framed photo of his wife laughing, apparently playing mini-golf, with their two daughters. Luc said, Andernos-les-Bains. They have a family house at Andernos-les-Bains. His wife is from Bordeaux. My head was beginning to spin a little. With a slowness bordering on the melodramatic, Luc started to unbutton his shirt with one hand. Then he pulled out his shirt tails. I understood that the idea was for me to follow suit, to strip at the same rhythm a few metres away. Luc Condamine exerts a real power over me in this respect. I was wearing a dress, and over it a cardigan. I revealed a shoulder. Then I shrugged off a cardigan sleeve to overtake him. Luc shrugged off one of his shirtsleeves. I removed the cardigan and threw it onto the floor. He did the same with his shirt. Luc was bare-chested now. He was smiling at me. I lifted up my dress and rolled down a stocking. Luc took off his shoes. I removed the other stocking, which I knotted into a ball and threw at him. Luc undid his flies. I paused for a moment. He freed his penis and I suddenly noticed that the sofa was turquoise. A sparkly turquoise beneath the artificial light of the alcove, and I thought that in view of everything else it was a rather surprising choice of colour for the sofa. I wondered who in this couple was responsible for the decor. Luc lay down in a lascivious position, which I found attractive and embarrassing at the same time. I looked around the room, at the paintings in their artificial gloom, the photos, the Moroccan lanterns. I wondered to whom the books, the guitar, the horrible elephant's foot belonged. I said, you'll never leave all this. Luc Condamine raised his head and stared at me as if I had just said something completely ludicrous.

Ernest Blot

My ashes. I don't know where they should go. Imprison them somewhere or scatter them? That's the question I ask myself, as I sit in the kitchen, in my dressing gown, in front of the laptop. Jeannette bustles back and forth, like a woman glad to spring into action on a public holiday. She opens cupboards, sets machines into motion, clatters the plates. I'm trying to read an electronic version of a newspaper. I say, Jeannette . . . ! Please. My wife replies, you don't have to stay in the kitchen while I'm getting breakfast ready. A rumble of inclement weather can be heard through the window. I feel worn out, stooped, and I'm frowning despite my specs. I stare at my hand straying across the table, gripping this gadget called a *mouse*; a body struggling against a world to which it no longer belongs. Oldies are people from another time placed in the future, my grandson Simon said the other day. A genius, that kid. The rain starts lashing against the window and my head is filled with pictures of the sea, of rivers, of ashes. My father was cremated. We picked him up in a metal box that was square, ugly, and painted the same brown as the colour of the classroom walls at the Collège Henri-Avril in Lamballe. I scattered his ashes with my sister Marguerite and two cousins on a bridge at Guernonze. He wanted to be in the River Braive. A hundred metres from the house where he was born. At six o'clock in the evening. In the heart of town. I was sixty-four. A few months after my quintuple heart bypass. There is no spot that bears his name. Marguerite can't come round to the idea that there's no way of locating him. When I go there (once a year, it's a long way), sometimes I steal a flower from a riverbank, and sometimes I buy one, which I throw in furtively. It floats away on the water. And I experience ten minutes of feeling whole. My father was frightened of being imprisoned like his brother. A brother who was his opposite. A large-scale gambler. A sort of Great Gatsby. When he walked into a restaurant, the staff would grovel. He was cremated as well. His last wife wanted to put him with her family, in their pharaoh's tomb. Some undertaker's minion prised the bronze sculpted door ajar, placed the urn on the first of twelve marble shelves, then closed it again. In the car, on the way back from the cemetery, my father said, your whole life you pride yourself on entering via the main entrance, but in the end they sneak you through a gap and fling you in haphazardly. I, Ernest, would also like to melt into the current. But since I sold Plou-Gouzan L'Ic, I don't have a river. As for my childhood river, it's no longer pleasant. It used to be wild, with herbs growing between the stones, and a wall of honeysuckle running alongside. Today, the banks have been concreted over, and there's a car park nearby. Or else into the sea. But it's too big (and I'm frightened of sharks). I want you to throw my ashes into a waterway, I tell Jeannette, but I haven't decided which one yet. Jeannette turns off the toaster. She wipes her hands on a tea towel that's lying around and sits down opposite me. – Your ashes? You want to be cremated, Ernest? Too much distress in her face. Too much pathos. Yes, I laugh, flashing my villainous teeth. – And you say it just like that, as if you were talking about the storm? – It's not a big topic of conversation. She goes quiet. She smooths the cloth on the table, you know I'm against it. – I know, but I don't want to be stacked in a vault, Jeannette. – You don't have to do as your father did. You're seventy-three. – It's the right age to do as one's father did. I put my specs back on. I say, would you be kind enough to let me read? You stab me and then you go back to your newspaper, she replies. I'd give anything for a newspaper to appear on my screen. I'm missing a password, a login, what do I know? Our daughter Odile has got it into her head that I need some kind of refresher course. She's frightened of my becoming rusty and isolated. When I was in office, nobody asked me to be in tune with modernity. Sinuous bodies flit about the screen. I am reminded of the flies that used to float before my eyes when I was a child. I had mentioned them to a little friend. Are they angels? I asked her. Yes, she told me. I had felt a degree of pride. I don't believe in anything. Certainly not in any religious nonsense. But a little bit in angels. In constellations. In my role, however infinitesimal, in the book of cause and effect. There's no law against imagining oneself as part of a whole. I don't know what Jeannette's up to with that tea towel instead of making the toast. She twists the corners and wraps them around her index finger. Which I find extremely distracting. I don't want to get into an argument with my wife. Making oneself understood is impossible. It can't be done. Particularly within the framework of matrimony, where everything lurches towards the criminal courts. Jeannette unfurls her tea towel in one clean movement and says gloomily, you don't want to be with me. With you where? I say. – With me, generally. – Of course I do, Jeannette, I want to be with you. – No. – In death each of us is alone. Stop it with the tea towel, what are you doing? – I've always found it sad that your parents aren't buried together. Your sister shares my sentiments. Father is very happy in the Braive, I say. And your mother is sad, says Jeannette. – My mother's sad! (My villainous teeth again.) All she had to do was follow him instead of having her parents' bodies reduced in order to have them join the family vault. Did anybody make her? – You are monstrous, Ernest. Nothing new there, I say. Jeannette would like to bury me alongside her so that passers-by might see our two names. Jeannette Blot and her devoted husband, safely stashed in stone. She would like to erase for ever the snubs of our conjugal life. In the old days, when I'd spent the night away, she would crumple my pyjamas before the maid arrived. My wife is counting on the grave to trump wagging tongues, she wishes to remain a *petite-bourgeoise* even in death. The rain is hammering the tiles. On my way home from Bréhau-Monge in Lamballe where my boarding school was, the evening wind would be blowing. I would thrust my nose into the teeming sky. There's that line from Renan: 'When the clock strikes five . . .' In which book? I'd like to read it again. Jeannette has stopped fiddling with the tea towel. She stares vacantly at the cloudy day. When she was young, there was something affronted about her. She looked like the actress Suzy Delair. Time also changes a face's soul. Aren't I even allowed a coffee? I say. She shrugs. I wonder what sort of day it'll turn out to be. I never used to pay any attention to this dizzying loop of day and night, I didn't even know whether it was morning, afternoon or God knows what time. I went to the Ministry, I went to the bank, I womanised, not once did I worry about the possible consequences. Occasionally I still feel elated enough for a spot of womanising, but after a certain age the preludes are tiring. Jeannette says, one can always choose to be cremated without having one's ashes scattered. I don't even look up. I return to my bogus cyber activity. I am not against learning something new, but to what purpose? To stimulate my brain cells, that's what my daughter says. Will it change my view of the world? There's already enough pollen and rubbish in the air without adding to it with the dust of death, it's not worth it, says Jeannette. I'll ask somebody else, I say. Odile, or Robert. Or Jean, but I'm worried the fool might depart this life before me. I didn't think he was in very good shape last Tuesday. Throw me into the Braive. I'll go and find my father. Just make sure that nobody inflicts any kind of ceremony on me, no funeral or other monkey business, no dull and solemn words. You never know, I might die before you, says Jeannette. – No, no, you're hardy. – If I die before you, Ernest, I want there to be a blessing and for you to talk about how you asked me to marry you in Roquebrune. Poor Jeannette. Back in a time that's now just a blurry haze, I asked for her hand through the spyhole of a medieval dungeon where I had imprisoned her. If she knew how Roquebrune has lost all meaning for me. How the past has dissolved and vanished into thin air. Two beings

69

live side by side but they are distanced by their imaginations more definitively each day. Women build enchanted palaces deep inside themselves. Somewhere in there you've been mummified without your knowledge. No liberties taken, no lack of scruples, no cruelty is construed as real. When the time for eternity comes, we will have to tell a tale of stripling youths. Everything is misunderstanding and torpor. – Don't count on it, Jeannette. I'll disappear before you happily. And you will attend my cremation. Don't worry, it doesn't smell of grilled pig any more the way it used to. Jeannette pushes back her chair and stands up. She throws her tea towel onto the table. She turns off the gas cooker where the water for my eggs is boiling and unplugs the toaster. As she leaves the room, she calls out to me, happily your father didn't choose to be cut up into little pieces, or you'd want to be cut up into little pieces too. I think she switches off the ceiling light. The day is radiating no light and I remain in what now feels like a dark closet. I take out the packet of Gauloises from my pocket. I had promised Doctor Ayoun not to smoke any more. Just as I had promised him to eat salad and grilled steaks. Nice chap, Ayoun. But one isn't going to kill me. My eyes land on the wooden shrimping net that's been hanging from the wall for an age. Fifty years ago, somebody used to dip it under the algae and in the cracks. In the old days. Jeannette used to store bunches of thyme, bay and all sorts of herbs in the net. Objects pile up and no longer serve any purpose. No more do we. I listen to the rain, which has dropped a tone. As has the wind. I tilt the lid of the computer. Everything that is before our eyes is already past. I am not sad. Things are made to disappear. I'll go on my way without any fuss. No coffin to be found, nor any bones. Everything will carry on as it's always done. Everything will depart merrily into the water.

Philip Chemla

I'd like to suffer for love. The other evening, at the theatre, I heard the lines: 'Sadness after intimate sexual intercourse one is familiar with of course . . . Yes, that one knows and is prepared to face.' It was in Beckett's *Happy Days*. Happy days of sadness unknown to me. I don't dream of a union, of an idyll, I don't dream of sentimental bliss, which may or may not endure, no, I'd like to be acquainted with a certain kind of sadness. I can imagine it. I may already have tasted it. A sensation halfway between loss and the heavy heart of childhood. Among the hundreds of bodies I desire, I'd like to land on the one with the gift to hurt me. Even from afar, even absent, even lying on a bed, with his back to me. On the lover armed with an imperceptible blade that nicks the skin. That's the hallmark of love, as I know from the books I used to read long ago before medicine robbed me of all my time. Between my brother and myself, there was never a word. When I was ten, he came into my bed. He was five years older than me. The door was ajar. I didn't fully understand what it meant but I knew it was forbidden. I don't recall what we used to do exactly. For years. Stroking, rubbing. I remember the day when he appeared, and my first orgasm. That's all. I'm not sure whether we kissed but judging by its place in my later life, he must have kissed me. Gradually, over time, right up until his marriage, I was the one who sought him out. Not a word between us. Apart from *no* when I appeared. He would say no, but he always gave in. Between my brother and me, I only recall the silences. No exchanges, no language to sustain an imaginary life. No overlap of emotion and sex. At the bottom of the garden, there was a garage. Through a broken window, I would watch life out in the street. One night, a dustman saw me and winked. Night-time, darkness, a forbidden man on his cart. Afterwards, when I wasn't so young, I would go out hunting dustmen. My father subscribed to *Living*

Africa. He had a brother in Guinea. It was my first porn magazine. Dark bodies on matt paper. Rugged peasants, guardians, almost naked, who glistened on the page. On a wall, above my bed, I had hung up Nefertiti. She watched over me like some dark untouchable icon. Before the Internet, I gave myself to the Arabs in the squares of the city. I would say, help yourself. One day, in a stairwell, as we were getting undressed, I sensed that the guy was going to steal my cash. I said, do you want some money? He melted into my arms. Things became simple, tender almost. My father has no knowledge of a whole aspect of my life. He's an upstanding man, with a strong sense of the father–son bond. A good Jew and true. I often think of him. I've felt freer since I began paying. My position is more legitimate, even though I have to redress the balance of power. I haggle with some of the boys. I worry about their lives, I treat them with respect. In secret I say to my father, yes, there is a little erring but the main path is adhered to. On Saturday evenings or sometimes in the week, after my consultations, when I don't have a meeting, I go to the woods, to the cinemas, to the places where I find the boys I'm after. I say to them, I like big cocks. I ask to see it. They get it out. It goes hard or not. For a while now, when I choose somebody, I want to know if he slaps. (I don't pay any more for a slap. The slap shouldn't be part of the deal.) Before, I used to ask this question when we were on our way. These days I ask upfront. The question isn't complete. The real one would be: do you slap? And immediately afterwards, do you console? But you can't ask that. Any more than you can say, console me. The furthest I can go is: stroke my face. I wouldn't dare say any more. Some words don't belong there. It's a strange command, *console me*. Among all the other commands, lick me, slap me, kiss me, use your tongue (many don't), it's impossible to imagine *console me*. What I really want can't be put into words. For my face to be hit, to offer up my face to his blows, to put my lips, my teeth, my eyes at his disposal, then suddenly to be stroked, when I'm least expecting it, and hit again with the right rhythm, at the right pace, and when I've climaxed, to be taken in his arms, carried, covered in kisses. That kind of perfection doesn't exist, or else it is beyond the love I know, perhaps. Since I started paying and can prescribe what takes place, I've been returned to myself. I do what I can't get in real life: I kneel down, I subjugate myself. I press my knees into the ground. I return to total submission. Money binds us like any other attachment. The Egyptian put his hands on my face. He took hold of my face, he placed his palms against my cheeks. This was what my mother used to do when I had earache, she tried to bring down the burning sensation of the fever with her hands. Otherwise, in everyday life, she was distant. The Egyptian licked my mouth, he disappeared into the night, like the dustmen of old. I've been looking for him ever since. I pace up and down the service road, I head into the woods. He's not there. If I try hard enough, I can still feel the moistness of his tongue on my lips. A vertiginous residue of something unknown to me. Jean Ehrenfried, a patient I've become attached to, gave me Rilke's *Duino Elegies*. He said to me, it's poetry, Doctor, perhaps you might have time? He opened the book in front of me and read out the opening words (as he did so I noticed that his voice had thinned since our last appointment), 'Who, if I cried out, might hear me – among the ranked Angels?' It's a slim volume. I have it by my bed. I read that line again while thinking of Ehrenfried's faint voice, his combination of polka-dot ties and fancy silk handkerchiefs. The poetry has been waiting for me beneath the bedside lamp for weeks. I rise at half past six every morning. I see my first patient an hour later. I can see thirty in a day. I teach, I write articles for international oncology and radiotherapy journals, I do fifteen conferences a year. I no longer have the time to put life in perspective. Friends drag me to the theatre sometimes. I saw *Happy Days* recently. A small parasol beneath an oppressive sun. The body slowly sinking, devoured by the ground, the being that wants to endure *with a light heart* and that rejoices in tiny surprises. This I recognise. I admire it every day. But I'm not sure I want to hear the other words. Poets have no sense of time. They lure you into a pointless gloom. I didn't ask the Egyptian for his phone number. In general, I don't ask. What for? I've taken the odd number. Not his. Somewhere on me he's left a mark I can't define. Perhaps it has to do with Beckett's evil genius. It isn't the Egyptian I'm searching for in the woods, behind the fencing in Passy. I've even searched in booths where I'd never seen him before. It's a whiff of sadness. Something intangible, something deeper than we can get a handle on, and which has nothing to do with reality. Mine's a good life. Every morning I rise on the dot.

I discovered that I was strong. By which I mean that I was suited to making decisions, taking risks. My patients have my mobile phone number, they can call me at any time. I owe them a great deal. I want to be worthy of them (for the same reason I want to keep up to date, and practise non-clinical cancer treatments as well). I've known for a long time that death exists. Before taking up medicine, there was already a clock inside my head. I'm not angry with my brother. I can't say exactly what place he occupies in my life. Human complexity can't be reduced to a causal principle. Perhaps without those years of silence I'd have been brave enough to face the abyss of a relationship that combines sex and love. Who can say? For the most part, I pay afterwards. Nearly always. The other person has to trust me, it's proof of friendship. But I paid the Egyptian first. By chance. He didn't put the note in his pocket, he kept it in his hand. The note was in my field of vision while I was sucking him off. He put it in my mouth. I sucked his dick and the money. He stuffed the note into my mouth and put his hand over my face. A pledge with no tomorrow that nobody will ever know about. When I was a child, I sometimes gave my mother a stone or a conker I found on the ground. I also used to sing her little songs. Offerings that were useless and everlasting. I've often had to convince my patients that the present is the only reality. The Egyptian boy put the note in my mouth and placed his hand on my face. I took everything he gave me, his cock, his money, his joy, his sorrow.

Loula Moreno

Anders Breivik, the Norwegian who shot sixty-nine people and killed eight others with a bomb, told an Oslo court, 'I'm a very nice person normally.' When I read those words I thought of Darius Ardashir straight away. Normally, when he's not trying to destroy me, Darius Ardashir is a very nice person too. Apart from me, his own wife maybe, and the women who've been unlucky enough to become attached to him, nobody knows he's a monster. The journalist who interviewed me this morning was the kind of woman who sips her tea with careful hand motions and a whole series of irritating rituals. Yesterday, towards six in the evening, Darius Ardashir said to me, I'll call you back in fifteen minutes. On the table, my mobile doesn't ring and it doesn't light up. It's midday. I almost went stir-crazy last night. The journalist said, you've just turned thirty, do you have a special wish? – I've got a hundred. – Give one example. I say, to play a nun. Or to have wavy hair. Appalling answers. I'm trying to be witty. I've got no idea how to keep things simple and on the surface. – A nun! She manufactures a rather twisted smile that's designed to confirm I wouldn't be first choice for the job. – Why not? – What's your chief weakness? – I've got thousands. – The one you'd like to get rid of? – My bad taste. – You've got bad taste? In which area? Men, I say. And instantly regret it. I always talk too much. Next to us, a kid is cleaning a table. She wipes a damp cloth over the polished wood in the correct circular motion, she moves the matchbox holder, she puts the *pâtisseries* menu on another table and then returns everything to its starting position and moves on. From where I am, I can see her up by the bar asking for another job. The actual waitress gives her a tray, onto which she's put promotional cards folded into a tent shape, she points out the empty tables, the girl dutifully arranges the cards next to the potted violets. I love her earnestness. The journalist says, do you have a type when it comes to men? I hear myself answering, dangerous and irrational males. I temper it with a little chuckle, don't write that down, I'm talking rubbish. – That's a shame. – I'm not attracted to smooth, handsome guys, the kind you get in *Mad Men*, I like them short and rough around the edges, bad-tempered-looking, the ones who don't say much. I could keep spinning out my answer but I nearly choke on an olive stone. I say, don't write all that. – I've written it. – Don't publish it, it's of no interest. – On the contrary. – I don't want to talk about myself like this. – Our readers will feel honoured, you're giving them a present. She readjusts her skirt under her bottom and calls for more hot water for her tea. I polish off the olives and order a second glass of vodka. I let myself be hoodwinked, I have no authority over these people. The journalist asks me if I've got a cold. I say, no, why? She thinks I've got a deeper voice in real life. She says I have a husky bedroom voice. I laugh stupidly. She thinks she's flattering me with this idiotic expression. On the table my mobile shows no sign of life. None. None. The girl moves calmly between the sofas, her chin well forward. – Where does Loula Moreno come from? It's not your real name? – It comes from a Charlie Odine song . . .

83

'Empty promises on the backs of envelopes / In the beds of shabby impresarios / Pretty Loula, wait at the palace gates / For the big day to come, for your grand scenarios . . .' – And does the big day come? – In the song? – No. Has it come for you? – Me neither. I finish my vodka and laugh. Thank heavens for laughter. It's a wild card. It works every single time. The kid heads off. She's become a child again with a raincoat and satchel. Just as she's disappearing behind the wood-framed glass door, I see Darius Ardashir walk in. I know this bar is a haunt of his. To be honest, I even chose this bar in the faint hope of seeing him. But Darius Ardashir isn't with his usual conspirators in dark suits and ties (I've never understood what he actually does, he's the kind of guy whose name is linked to politics one day, and some industrial group or an arms deal the next), he's with a woman. I down my drink in one and set fire to my throat. I'm not used to drinking. Especially not in the morning. The woman is your tall, classic type with a blonde chignon. Darius Ardashir leads her towards an L-shaped sofa, next to the piano. His hair is wet. He places his hand on the small of her back. I haven't heard the journalist's question. I say, sorry, what was that? I raise my arm in the waiter's direction,

I order another vodka. I say to the journalist, it wakes me up, I didn't sleep much last night. I've always got to justify myself. It's insane. I'm thirty, I'm famous, I can dance on any precipice I like. Darius Ardashir is trying to close a small, patterned umbrella. He's struggling unintelligently with the ribs. In the end he flattens the spokes by force and wraps the fabric any which way. The woman laughs. The scene kills me. The journalist says, are you nostalgic about your childhood? From the way she's leaning towards me, as one might a deaf person, I'm guessing she's already asked me this question at least once. Oh, no, not at all, I say, I didn't enjoy being a child, I wanted to grow up. She leans in even more, she mutters something I can't hear, I take my mobile, I stand up, I say, will you excuse me a second? I head for the toilets as inconspicuously as possible. I'm swaying slightly because of the vodka. I look at myself in the mirror. I'm pale, I approve of the shadows under my eyes. I'm a good-looking girl. On my mobile I write, 'I can see you.' I send the message to Darius Ardashir. A few days ago, I told him I was his slave and that I wanted him to keep me on a leash. Darius Ardashir said he didn't like to feel encumbered and that even a briefcase got in his way. Carelessly I head back into the room. I don't look over towards the piano. When the journalist sees me returning, her face lights up with an almost maternal glow. Shall we carry on? she asks. I say, yes. I sit down. He must have seen my message, Darius Ardashir is addicted to his phone. I arch my back, I stretch my swan's neck. Whatever I do, I mustn't glance his way. The journalist rifles through her notes and says, you said . . . – God help me . . . – You said, men are love's guests. – I said that? – Yes. – Not bad. – Could you elaborate? I say, will somebody give me a hard time if I smoke? She says, probably. My mobile lights up. Darius A. is answering. 'Hey sexy.' I turn around. Darius Ardashir is ordering some drinks. He's wearing a brown jacket over a beige shirt, the blonde woman is in love with him, it's glaringly obvious. *Hey sexy*, as if nothing were happening. Darius Ardashir is a genius of the present moment. Night erases all trace of the previous day and words bounce as lightly as helium balloons. I send: 'Who is she?' Which I instantly regret. I write, 'No, I don't care.' Luckily I delete that. The journalist sighs and flops against the back of the chair. I write, 'We were meant to have dinner together last night – weren't we?!' Delete, delete. Reproaches make men run in the opposite direction. At the beginning,

Darius Ardashir used to say to me, I love you with my head, my heart and my cock. I repeated this to Rémi Grobe, my best friend, who said, your guy's a poet, I'll try it out, it should work with the odd fruitcake. With me it works just fine. I'm not into anything too subtle. I say to the journalist, what were we talking about? She shakes her head, she's lost track herself. I signal to the waiter, and ask for another bowl of nibbles with plenty of cashew nuts. I'm not going to leave it at *Who is she?* It's too weak. Especially as he's not answering. I write, 'Tell her you only like beginnings.' Brilliant. I'll send it. No, I won't. I'll go one better. I call the waiter over again. He arrives with some crisps and the cashew-nut mix. I ask him for a piece of paper. I say to the journalist, sorry it's a bit scrappy this morning. She raises a floppy hand as if giving up all hope. I haven't got time to feel embarrassed by this. The waiter brings me a sheet of printer paper. I ask him to wait. I write my line at the top of the page and carefully fold it over. I ask the waiter to hand it discreetly to the man in the brown jacket sitting near the piano, without disclosing its provenance. The boy says in a voice that's cringingly clear, Monsieur Ardashir? I flutter an eyelash to confirm. Off he goes. I tuck into the cashew mix. I've got to avoid looking at what's happening over by the piano at all costs. The journalist has emerged from her torpor. She's removed her glasses and is putting them back in their case. She is also starting to tidy away her notes. I don't want to be abandoned here, not now. I say to her, you know something, I feel old. You don't feel young when you're thirty. Last night, I couldn't sleep, I read Pavese's diary. Do you know it? I've got it on my bedside table, it's good to read sad things. There's a line where he says: 'the madmen, the cursed were children too, they played like you, they believed that something wonderful was waiting for them'. Don't write this, but for a long time I've thought my career would only ever be a meteoric flash. The journalist gives me a worried look. She's kind, poor thing. The boy returns with the piece of folded paper. I tremble. I hold it for a moment and then I unfold it. At the top is my line, 'Tell her you only like beginnings,' below, in his fine black hand, he's written 'Not always'. Nothing else. No full stop. Who do these words refer to? Me? The woman . . . ? I turn my head in the direction of the piano. Darius Ardashir and the woman are very jolly. The journalist leans in to me and says, something wonderful was waiting for you, Loula.

Raoul Barnèche

I ate a king of clubs. Not all of it, but nearly all. I'm a man who went to the extreme of putting a king of clubs in his mouth, ripping off part of it, chewing it the way a savage would chew raw flesh and swallowing it. That's what I did. I ate a card handled by dozens of others before me, in mid-tournament at Juan-les-Pins. The only thing I'll concede is my original mistake. Playing with Hélène. Letting myself be sweet-talked by women and their sentimental music. For years I've known not to play with my wife Hélène as my partner. The period when we could do so in a spirit of harmony (the word's exaggerated and doesn't exist in bridge), let's say of indulgence, or at any rate on my part, in a spirit, how can I put it, of conciliation, has long since passed. We did once win the French Open Mixed Pairs Championships, by a stroke of good luck. Since then, our partnership has failed to produce a single spark but it's wreaked havoc on my arteries. Hélène didn't know how to play bridge when I met her. A pal brought her to the café where we used to play at night. She was doing secretarial studies. She sat down, and she watched. Then she came back. I taught her everything. My father was a tool-making technician at Renault and my mother was a seamstress. Hélène came from the north. Her parents were textile workers. Things are more democratic now, but back then there weren't people like us in the clubs. Before I gave it all up for the game, I was a chemical engineer with Labinal. Days at Saint-Ouen, evenings at the Darcey, place Clichy, then after that the clubs. Weekends at the racecourse. Young Hélène would follow. You can't explain a passion for cards. It's like a separate pigeonhole in the brain. There's a pigeonhole marked *cards*. You've either got it or you haven't. You can take all the lessons in the world, nothing doing. Hélène had it. Short distance, she played honourably. Women can't concentrate long haul. After thirteen years of playing bridge separately, one fine morning Hélène wakes up and suggests we play the Juan-les-Pins tournament together again. Juan-les-Pins, blue sky, sea, memories of the *auberge* at Cannet, God knows what she was picturing. I should have said no, but I said yes, like all men in their dotage. The drama happened on the seventeenth board. Five spades bid by north–south. I lead the two of diamonds, dummy plays low, ace from Hélène, declarer plays low. Hélène plays her ace of clubs, declarer plays low, I've got three clubs to the king, I play the nine, small one from dummy. What does Hélène lead next? What does the woman go and do when I've taught her everything and she's become a so-called first-rank player? She plays another diamond. I'd played the nine of clubs, and Hélène plays another diamond! We had the top three of the suit, but we only made two of them. At the end of the hand, I displayed my king of clubs and I shouted, so what am I meant to do with this? Gobble it? D'you want me dead, Hélène? D'you want me to have a fit in the middle of this conference centre? I waved the card under her nose and stuffed it into my mouth. As I started chewing, I said, you saw my nine of clubs, you idiot, you think I played the nine for fun? Hélène was petrified. Our opponents were petrified. That fired me up. Eating card makes you want to throw up, but I got my jaws going and I concentrated on chewing. I noticed some movement around us, I heard somebody laugh, I saw the face of my friend Yorgos Katos getting closer, a guy from our place Clichy days. Yorgos said, what the hell are you doing, Raoul, come on spit that shit out, old pal. I said, with considerable difficulty, because I was determined to force down my king of clubs, where did she put her white stick? Eh? Show us your white stick, old girl! Yorgos said (or I think he did), you're not going to get all worked up for a tournament, Raoul, a beach game. Those are the last words I remember. I heard somebody calling the tournament director, the table swayed, Hélène stood up, held out her arms, I tried to grab hold of her fingers, I saw her floating with the others in a circle above my head, I felt bodies against me, I gagged, I threw up on the baize, and then nothing. I woke up in a room with lime-green walls I didn't recognise but which turned out to be our hotel room. Three people were whispering over by the door. Yorgos, Hélène and a stranger. Then the stranger left. Yorgos glanced over towards the bed and said, he's stirring.

Yorgos has the same hair as Joseph Kessel. A sort of lion's mane that attracts women and makes me jealous. Hélène rushed over to my bedside. – All right? She stroked my forehead gently. I said, what's going on? – Don't you remember? You got hysterical last night, during the tournament. You ate a king of clubs, said Yorgos. I ate a king of clubs? I said, trying to sit up and finding it a monumental effort. Hélène plumped my pillows. A ray of sunlight caught her face, she was as pretty as ever. I said, my little Bilette. She smiled at me, the doctor gave you a sedative injection, Rouli (we call each other Bilette and Rouli in private). Yorgos opened the window. We heard the sounds of children shouting and music from a merry-go-round. And I got a sudden rush, I don't know why, of buried images, the empty merry-go-round at the seaside resort where we used to go when I was a kid, the barrel organ, the grey weather. We stayed on a campsite. At the end of the day I would wait under the awning of the refreshment stall, watching the animals go round and round. A wave of sadness hit me. I thought, whoa steady on, what's that crazy doctor given me? I'll leave you, said Yorgos. You've got to stay in bed today. Tomorrow you can go for a walk. A bit of nature'll do you good, a blast of sea air. We met at a bistro on the corner of boulevard des Batignolles, Yorgos and me. We were twenty. When the Darcey closed, at two in the morning, we would move on to Pont Cardinet. We carried on like that for our whole lives without worrying about daylight. Club to bed and bed to club. We played everything, poker, backgammon, we fleeced a few suckers in back rooms. When it came to bridge, we had a laugh, we did the big international championships. He was the last person who should be recommending I take in some nature and a walk. He might as well have ordered my grave. I said, what happened? Is it serious? Don't you remember, Rouli? said Hélène. I replied, not clearly. Yorgos said, good luck, my dear. He kissed Hélène and off he went. Hélène brought me a glass of water. She said, you lost your temper at the end of a board. – Why aren't we at the tournament? – We got kicked out. I don't know what it is with merry-go-round music, but those hurdy-gurdies make such a racket. I said, close the window, Bilette, and the curtains too, I'm going to sleep a bit longer. The next day, towards noon, I woke up for good when Hélène got back from town with some packages and a new pink straw hat. She thought I looked much better. And she seemed thrilled with her purchases. She said, what d'you think, not too big? They had ones with ribbons on as well. I can change it, we need to go back and buy one for you in any case. I said, a straw hat like the old men, what next? Hélène said, the sun's strong, you're not going to get sunstroke on top of everything else. An hour later, I was sitting on a café terrace in the old town, with new glasses and a woven hat. Hélène had bought a guidebook and was letting herself get carried away with each new page. I, meanwhile, was discreetly ticking the horses I liked the look of in *Paris Turf* (I'd been allowed to buy it but not to consult it). She was the one who brought it up again. All of a sudden, she said, I didn't appreciate your calling me an idiot in front of everybody. – I called you an idiot, my Bilette? – In front of everybody. And she pouted like an upset child. That's no good at all, I said. – And the white stick, that was positively horrible, nobody says to their wife, show us your white stick, old girl, in front of five hundred people. – In front of five hundred people, come off it. – Everybody knows about it. – I wasn't myself, Bilette, you could see that. – All the same, it's alarming that you went ahead and ate the card. I shrugged and tucked my chin in like a man ashamed. It was hot. People were walking past with loose clothes and canvas bags, children eating ice creams, girls covered in charm bracelets. I couldn't think of anything to say to Hélène. I was watching the world go by, colourful and drab. Hélène said, how about we visit the Square Fort? Or the Archaeological Museum? – All right. Which one? said Hélène. – Whichever you prefer. – The Archaeological Museum, perhaps. They've got objects recovered from Greek and Phoenician ships. Vases, jewels. – Great. As we turned into a nearby street, I noticed a bistro showing live racing. I said, Bilette, how about we go our separate ways for an hour or so? Hélène said, if you set foot inside that bar, I'll go straight back to Paris. She grabbed the rolled-up copy of *Paris Turf* from my pocket and started waving it about in every direction. What's the point of being married if we don't do anything together? What's the point? – The Phoenicians bore me, Bilette. – If the Phoenicians bore you, then you shouldn't have ruined our tournament. – I wasn't the one who ruined the tournament. – It wasn't you? You're not the one who went mad, who insulted me and then vomited? – It was me. But not without reason. We had veered into the road and a car beeped its horn loudly. Hélène smacked the newspaper down on the bonnet. The guy swore at her through the window, she shouted, get stuffed! I tried to grab hold of her arm to drag her back onto the pavement but she wasn't having it. – You led the deuce of diamonds, Raoul, I thought you had an honour in diamonds. – If I wanted you to play diamonds again, I would play the two of clubs. – How am I supposed to know you've got three to the king? – You don't, but when you see me playing the nine, you must realise it's a signal. What's it called, Hélène, when your partner plays a nine? SIG-NAL. – I misinterpreted it. – You didn't misinterpret it, you don't look at the cards, you haven't looked at the cards for years. – How would you know, you don't play with me any more! – And with good cause! By this time there was a small gathering around us. Hélène's pink straw hat was too big (she was right about that) and I felt faintly ridiculous in mine. Hélène was bleary-eyed and her nose was starting to turn red. I noticed the Provençal-style earrings she must have bought herself. I felt a sudden rush of tenderness for the diminutive woman of my life and I said, sorry, my Bilette, I'm getting all worked up about nothing, come on, let's go to your museum, it'll do me good to see the amphora and all that jazz. While I was steering her (and waving off the onlookers), Hélène said, if old stones bore you, Rouli, shall we go somewhere else? They don't bore me at all, I said, now watch this. Solemnly, I took back my copy of *Paris Turf* and I threw it into a bin. While we were walking through the crowded back streets, arms around each other's waists, I said, and then afterwards we'll take a stroll over to the casino. It opens at four o'clock. If you don't want to stay with me at the blackjack table, you could go and play boule instead, my Bilette.

Virginie Déruelle

From the stairs, I could already hear Edith Piaf wailing. I
don't know how the other residents put up with the
volume. I can't bear that miserable voice and those *rrr*s
rolled in the throat. It's oppressive. My great-aunt is in a
nursing home. Or, I should say, a nursing bedroom because
she hardly ever comes out of it, and if I were her I'd do the
same. She makes crocheted patchworks. Bedspreads,
pillowcases and pointless squares. Not that there's any
point in any of them because my aunt's creations are
ghastly, outdated dust-traps. You pretend you're glad to
take them, but as soon as you're back home you stuff them
to the back of a cupboard. We're all too superstitious to

throw them away but we can't find anybody to give them to. Recently, a CD player was set up for her, which she can easily use. She loves Tino Rossi. But she also listens to Edith Piaf and some Yves Montand songs. When I walked into her bedroom, my great-aunt was trying to water a cactus by flooding the little table while Piaf bellowed: '*J'irais jusqu'au bout du monde / Je me ferais teindre en blonde / Si tu me le demandais . . .*'* I instantly turned it down and I said, Marie-Paule, cactuses don't need much water. Not this one, said my great-aunt, this one loves water, did you just turn off 'Hymne à l'amour'? – I didn't turn it off, I just lowered the volume. – How are you, my dear? Goodness gracious, don't go falling flat on your face in those shoes, my word you're perched high! – You're the one who's shrinking Marie-Paule. – It's just as well I'm shrinking, you've seen where I live. '*Je renierais ma patrie / Je renierais mes amis / Si tu me le demandais . . .*'** I switch off the music. I say, she gets on my nerves. Who? says my aunt, Cora Vaucaire? – That's not Cora Vaucaire, Marie-Paule, it's Edith Piaf. – Nonsense, it's

---

* 'I'd go to the ends of the world / I'd dye my hair blonde / If you asked me to . . .'
** 'I'd deny my fatherland / I'd deny my friends / If you asked me to . . .'

Cora Vaucaire. 'Hymne à l'amour' is Cora Vaucaire, I've still got my head screwed on, says my aunt. All right, if you like. But it's the song that gets on my nerves, I'm against love songs, I say. The better known they become, the more stupid they are. If I were queen of the world, I'd ban them. My aunt shrugs, who knows what you young people enjoy today. Would you like some orange juice, Virginie? She points to a bottle that's already been opened, started a thousand years ago. I pass on the offer and say, young people today go mad for love songs. All the singers do them, it's only me they annoy. You'll change your mind the day you meet a nice boy, says my aunt. She's managed to get up my nose in thirty seconds. As fast as my mother. It must be a trait of the women in my family. On the bedside table, there's a framed photo of her husband smoking a pipe. One day she showed me his drawer in the tallboy. She's kept all his letters, his words, his gifts. I don't have a clear recollection of my great-uncle, I was so young when he died. I sit down. I let myself collapse into the big flabby armchair that takes up too much space. It's a sad bedroom. Too many things, too much furniture. I get the balls of thread she had asked for out of my bag.

She hastily tidies them into the basket at the foot of her bed. She sits in the other chair. She says, right, now tell me some of your news. When she's got all her wits about her, I don't understand what she's doing here, alone, in this prison camp, far from everything. From time to time, on the telephone, it sounds like she's just been crying. But since the incident with the exploding rice dish, I know that my aunt's got her head screwed on, as she puts it, less and less. The last time my parents and I went round to her place, my aunt had put a glass dish full of cooked rice on a hotplate two hours before dinner. But no matter how much it was heated up, the rice on the top stayed cold. My aunt had just stirred it with a spatula, in other words she'd spilled it all over the worktop. Giving her any advice was out of the question, as was going into the kitchen. At one point, we glimpsed her through the gap in the door, up to her arms in rice, which she was kneading like she was shampooing a dog with scabies. At eight o'clock, the dish exploded, studding the kitchen with grains and shards. It was after this incident that my parents decided to put her in a home. I say, did you like Raymond being a pipe smoker? – Did he smoke a pipe? – In the photo he's smoking a pipe. – Oh, he used to adopt a new look, from time to time. And I couldn't keep tabs on everything, you know. When are you going to get married, my dear? I'm twenty-five, Marie-Paule, I say, I've got plenty of time. She says, would you like some orange juice? – No thanks. I ask her, were you faithful? She laughs. She raises her eyes to the ceiling and says, a leather salesman, think about it, I didn't really mind, you know! With some people, you can't see the face of their youth. It's got worn away with the years. And with others, it's the opposite, they light up like kids. I see it in the clinic with the seriously ill. And with my Auntie Marie-Paule. – Was Raymond the chatty type? She thinks about this, and then she says, no, not really. A man doesn't need to be chatty. I say, you're not wrong. She winds a scrap of wool around her fingers, I've still got my head screwed on, you know. – I know you've got your head screwed on, speaking of which I'd like you to give me your opinion about something important. She says, right you are. Would you like some orange juice? I say, no thanks. Here we go. You remember I'm a medical secretary? – You're a medical secretary, yes, yes. – I work in a clinic with two cancer specialists. – Yes, yes. – And there's one of Doctor Chemla's patients, she's your age, who always comes with her son. What a nice man, says my aunt. – He's very nice. Especially given what a pain his mother is. He's old. For all I know, he might even be forty. But I like them old. I get bored with boys my age. One day I found myself smoking a cigarette outside with him. To tell you the truth, I'd noticed him for a while. Let me describe him to you: he's dark, not very tall, he looks like a less handsome version of, d'you know the actor Joaquin Phoenix? A Spaniard, says my aunt. – Yes . . . whatever. So, we're smoking, under the awning. I smile at him. He smiles back. There we are, smoking and smiling. I try to make my cigarette last but I finish it before him. Seeing as I'm at work, in my white coat, I've got no reason to hang around. I say to him, see you later, and I go back to my basement. As the months pass and the consultations go by, I exchange a few words with him. I plan the appointments, I find the addresses for ancillary care services. One day, his mother gives me chocolates, she says, it was Vincent who chose them, another time, I see him in front of a lift that's not coming and I show him the staff lift, you know that kind of thing. On the days when

Zawada (that's their surname) is written in the book, I feel happy, I make a special effort with my make-up. Would you like a glass of orange juice? says my aunt. – No, thanks. He's called Vincent Zawada. Don't you think that's a nice name? Yes it is, says my aunt. – At the moment, it's like a dream, they're coming every week because she's having radiotherapy. On Monday, there we were again, him and me, under the awning smoking. This time, I got there after. He's like Raymond. Not at all chatty. My aunt nods. She's listening to me quietly, one hand on top of the other in her lap. From time to time, she glances outside. Just in front of her window, there are two poplar trees that partially hide the buildings opposite. I say, I take my courage in both hands and I dare to ask him what he does. You see, it's sort of weird, a man who's always free in the daytime. My aunt says, quite, quite. She stares with her midnight-blue eyes. She can run a thread through the eye of a tiny needle without glasses. I say, he's in music. He's a pianist and he composes as well. After a bit, he finishes his cigarette. And then, instead of going back to his mother in the waiting room, for no reason, because we're not talking at this point, he stays there. He waits for me. There's no reason to stay outside, agreed? My aunt nods. Especially when it's cold and nasty. We stay there, the two of us, like the first time, smiling at each other. I can't think of anything to say. I go all shy with this guy even though I'm generally quite forthright. When I finish my cigarette, he pushes the glass door to let me through in front of him (which proves he waited for me), and he says, let's take your lift. We could each have taken a different lift, or he could have said nothing, right? Let's take your lift, don't you think that's a way of bringing us together? I say. My aunt says, I do think. In the lift, which is a hospital bed lift, and very deep, he stands next to me, as if the lift was tiny. I promise you, Marie-Paule, I say to my aunt, I can't say he glues himself to me but, given the size of the lift, he stands really close. Unfortunately, it's quick from the ground floor to minus two. Down there, we walk a little way together, then he goes back into the waiting room, and I head to the secretarial offices. Almost nothing had happened, or nothing in particular, but when we went our separate ways, at the point where the two corridors meet, I felt like we were leaving one another on a train platform, after a secret journey. D'you think I'm in love, Marie-Paule? Well, yes, you do seem to be, says my aunt. – You know, I've never been in love. Or just for two hours. Two hours, that's not long, says my aunt. – So what am I meant to do now? If I rely on us bumping into each other at the clinic, we'll reach a standstill. Between the patients, the telephone, writing up consultations, I'm simply not available at the clinic. No, says my aunt. – D'you think he likes me? Is it obvious he likes me? He likes you for sure, says my aunt, is he Spanish? Beware of Spaniards. – No, he's not Spanish! – Thank goodness for that. My aunt gets up and goes over to the window. The trees are moving in the wind. They sway together, and the branches and leaves are going berserk in the same direction. She says, look at my poplars. Look at what fun they're having. Have you seen where they've put me. Luckily, I've got my two tall friends over there. They cover my windowsill with their seeds, you know their little caterpillars, that attract the birds. Don't you want some orange juice? No thanks, Marie-Paule, I say, I've got to go now. My aunt gets up and rummages around in her wool basket. She says, could you bring me a ball of Diana-Noel wool, green, like this one? I say, yes of course. I give her a hug. She's tiny, my Auntie Marie-Paule.

It breaks my heart to leave her there, all alone. On the stairs, I can hear Edith Piaf again. It sounds like somebody's singing with her. I climb back up a few steps and I can make out, above the rousing music, my aunt's frail voice: '*C'est inouï, quand même / T'en fais jamais trop / T'es l'homme, t'es l'homme, t'es l'homme / T'es l'homme qu'il me faut.*'*

---

* 'It's incredible, all the same . You never go too far / You' re the man, you're the man, you're the man / You're the man that I need.'

Rémi Grobe

Who am I meant to be? I had asked her. – A colleague. – A colleague? I'm not a lawyer. A journalist, said Odile. – Like your husband? – Why not? – Which newspaper? – Something serious. *Les Echos*. Nobody reads it over there. When we arrived in Wandermines, Odile wanted me to park the car in a small street behind the place de l'Eglise. I said, it's raining. – I can't turn up in a BMW. – Of course you can, the boss's lawyer will be in a Beamer too, it's perfect. She couldn't make up her mind. She had dolled herself up, higher heels than usual, classic hairdo. I said, you look smart, you're the Parisian lady, d'you really think they want to be represented by a gaucho in clogs? She said, all right then. I think she mainly said all right then because of the rain. I parked on the square. I walked round to the other side of the car with the umbrella. She got out. Small, sheathed in her coat with the scarf knotted around her neck, a stiff handbag and a satchel for files. That was when I started to feel something, as in something real. While we were getting out of the car, in Wandermines, in the rain. We don't talk enough about the influence of place on our affections. Waves of nostalgia rise to the surface without warning. Beings change their natures, just like in the storybooks. In front of the church half disappearing into the fog, in front of the red-brick buildings and the chip stall, I watched the leading lawyer for victims of asbestos, a girl who was unsure of herself and laughing (I adore her laugh) as she recognised those welcoming her. In the midst of this brotherhood dressed up in Sunday best, hurrying towards the civic hall so as to escape the rain, while I was holding Odile's arm to help her across the slippery church square, I experienced the catastrophe of emotion. That kind of foolishness had always been out of the question. I know her husband, she knows the women who come and go in my life. There's never been anything at stake between us apart from a bit of sexual fun. I thought, you're losing your grip here, buddy, but it'll pass. In the civic hall, Odile addressed three hundred people, the workers and their families. At the end of her speech, everybody applauded. The chairwoman of the Victims' Association said to her, you've filled three coaches for Thursday's demo. Odile whispered in my ear, I was made to go into politics. Her face was scarlet. I nearly told her politics requires a cooler head than hers, but I stopped myself. We left the main meeting room for another room laid out for the official banquet. By three o'clock in the afternoon, we were still on the fizz. A plump woman in her sixties presided in a pleated skirt. There was a PA system that would have been state of the art in the eighties. I got friendly with a former asbestos mould-stripper, a guy with cancer of the pleura. He told me about his life, the corrugated sheets cut into pieces, the pipes that were ground and sanded down without protection. The asbestos storeroom, the dust. He told me, we used to take delivery of the asbestos in tins, we played with it like it was snow. I could see Odile dancing the Madison with some widows (she's the one who called it the Madison, I don't know the first thing when it comes to dance), as well as a sort of tango with some men kitted out with oxygen cylinders. A woman called out, you look like you're having a bad hair day, Odile, you should get a perm! I thought, this is real life, trestle tables, fraternity, dust, Odile Toscano dancing in a function room. Rémi, I thought, this is what you should have done in life, mayor of Wandermines, in Nord-Pas-de-Calais, with its church, its factory, its cemetery. The coq au vin was brought out in big pots. My pal told me there were more people freshly buried in the cemetery than there were inhabitants living in the commune. He said, we're putting up a fight. I thought about the power of the word. He said, when my brother died, I had them sing 'Le Temps des Cerises'. My head was about to explode. When the day was over, it was me who offered to drive us back to Douai even though I was as sloshed as Odile. In the hotel room, Odile collapsed onto the bed. She said, I'm a wreck, Rémi, I can't call the kids in this state, have you got any aspirin? – I've got better than that. And I fetched a small bottle of cognac from the minibar. I was a wreck too, plus I was still feeling unhinged. The way she lay there, a pillow tucked under her head, swigging the cognac. Her laughter, her exhausted face. I thought, she's mine.

Maître Toscano, my own little lawyer. I lay on top of her, I kissed her, undressed her, we made love with hangovers and just the right amount of pain. Around ten, we felt hungry. The hotel recommended a restaurant that would still be open at that time of night. We wandered through Douai before finding it. We walked along a river which Odile told me was called the Scarpe, I don't know why the name has stuck in my head, she told me other stuff about the buildings, she showed me the law courts. It was windy and there was a damp drizzle, but I liked the impenetrable mood, the silence, the funny street lamps, I was ready to stay on and live there. Odile walked boldly, her nose swollen with the cold. I felt the urge to wrap my arms around her, to hold her tightly, but I held back. That kind of foolishness had always been out of the question between us. In the restaurant, we ordered vegetable soup and ham on the bone. Odile wanted tea and me a beer. She said, you shouldn't drink any more alcohol. I said, it's nice of you to take care of me. She smiled. I said, those people really made an impression on me. I lead a bloody stupid life. I only see spineless fools. She said, not everybody's lucky enough to be born in a mining basin. – You've made an impression on me too. Ah, at last! said Odile and she gestured for me to elaborate. – You get involved, you show solidarity, you're strong. You're beautiful. – Rémi? Hello? Are you okay? – I mean it, you're fighting with them, for them. – It's my job. – You could do it differently. Be more aloof. The workers love you. Odile laughed (I've already said I adore her laugh). – The workers love me! The people love me, I told you, I should go into politics. As for you, you're going to sleep well tonight, my poor darling. – You're wrong to laugh. I'm serious. The way you danced, and cleared the plates, your comforting words, you made the day magical. – You didn't think I looked too podgy in those trousers? – No. – D'you think I look like I'm having a bad hair day? – Yes. But I prefer it to the helmet look this morning. In a flash I thought, tomorrow we'll be in Paris. Tomorrow evening, Odile will be back home, in her cosy cell, with the children and the husband. The devil knows where I'll be. Normally it wouldn't matter, but with things taking an unusual turn, I thought, you'd better watch your back, buddy. I took my mobile out of my pocket, I said to Odile, excuse me, and I searched for Loula Moreno. She's beautiful, funny and desperate. Exactly what I need. I

114

wrote, 'Free tomorrow evening?' Odile was blowing on her soup. I felt a mounting sense of panic. Fear of abandonment. As a child, my parents would leave me with other people. I used to keep very still, getting smaller and smaller in the gloom. My mobile lit up and I read: 'Free tomorrow evening, my angel, but you'll have to come to Klosterneuburg.' I remembered that Loula was filming in Austria. Who else? Everything okay? asked Odile. Very much so, I said. – You look annoyed. – Just a client postponing a meeting, nothing important. And then I asked in an offhand kind of way, what are you doing tomorrow evening? We're celebrating my mother's seventieth birthday, Odile replied. – At your place? – No, my parents' home, in Boulogne. It does her good to have people over. Doing the shopping, cooking for everybody. I worry about my parents sinking deeper into their gloom. – Don't they do anything? – My father's a Treasury auditor, he was on Raymond Barre's staff at the Matignon, before heading up the Wurmster Bank. Ernest Blot, ring any bells? – Vaguely. – He had to wind down because of a cardiac problem. Now he's chair of the board of directors but it's honorary. He does a bit of charity work, marks time. My mother, nothing. She feels lonely. My father is odious. They should have separated long ago. Odile has drunk her tea, scooped the slice of lemon from the bottom of her cup and removed the surrounding peel. One of the side effects of feeling emotionally unhinged is that nothing washes over you any more. Everything becomes a sign, everything is material to be decrypted. I was rash enough to imagine her last words might contain a message and I said, have you ever thought about separating, your husband and you? I instantly covered her face with my hands and said, I don't care, forget I ever mentioned it, I couldn't care less. When I took my hands away, Odile said, he must think about it every day, I'm foul. I said, I bet you are. Robert's foul too, but he knows how to win me back, she said, swallowing the lemon. I didn't like her choosing the same meaningless word for both of them, I didn't like her saying *Robert*, Robert's name bursting into our conversation. It annoyed me that she let me glimpse their life, which I couldn't care less about, in such a trivial way. It's foolish to think that emotions bring us closer together, quite the reverse, they sanction the distance between us. Throughout the day, fizzing with energy, in the rain, on the stage with her mic, in the car, in the hotel room with the curtains drawn, Odile had never seemed more than a face away, a caress away. But in this dreary half-empty restaurant where, against my better judgement, I had begun clocking the tiniest gesture, the tone of each word, with febrile attentiveness, she slipped away, she vanished into a world in which I had no part. I said, I'd shoot myself after two days if I had to live here. Odile laughed (a laugh that sounded sharp and contractual to my ear). – Ten minutes ago you claimed the opposite. You were all up for Douai. – I've changed my mind. I'd shoot myself. She shrugged. She dunked some bread in what remained of the lacklustre soup. I sensed that she was almost bored. I was almost bored too, overcome by the moroseness of lovers when there's nothing else happening beyond bed. I couldn't think of anything to say. I heard the rain returning and knocking at the window. Odile looked dismayed and said, we didn't bring the umbrella! I thought of the mould-stripper laughing with his thoroughly stained teeth, of the organiser in her unflattering pleated skirt, and, God knows why, of my father, a coach-builder, at Porte de Pantin, who used to curse the metalwork because the sunroof leaked. I was tempted to tell Odile about this, but only for half a second.

117

I scrolled through the list of contacts on my mobile and landed on Yorgos Katos. I thought, that's it, go and lose your shirt at poker, buddy. I wrote, 'Need a sucker at the table tomorrow night? A few grand to blow.' Who are you writing to? said Odile. – Yorgos Katos. Have I never told you about Yorgos? – Never. – A friend who earns his living at cards. One day, years ago, he was playing with Omar Sharif in a bridge tournament. He could feel a swarm of girls clustered behind his back. He thought to himself, they know I'm a much better player than he is. Not for one second did it occur to him that they wanted to be face-to-face with Omar Sharif. Odile said she was in love with the desert prince from *Lawrence of Arabia*. For her, Omar Sharif was in a turban, on a black steed, and not wedged in at a bridge table. I couldn't have agreed with her more. My mood lifted again. Everything was falling back into place.

Chantal Audouin

A man's a man. There's no such thing as a married man, or a man off limits. He doesn't exist (as I explained to Doctor Lorrain when I was sectioned). When you meet somebody, you're not interested in his marital status. Or his emotional state. Emotions are fickle and mortal. Like everything on earth. Beasts die. Plants too. From one year to the next, streams are not the same. Nothing lasts. People want to believe the opposite. They spend their lives sticking the pieces back together again and calling it marriage, fidelity or I don't know what. I can't be bothered with such nonsense any more. I try my luck according to what I fancy. I'm not afraid of falling on my face. I've got nothing to lose. I won't be beautiful for ever. The mirror is less and less friendly, as it is. One day, the wife of Jacques Ecoupaud, the minister, my lover, rang me to arrange for us to meet. I was stunned. She must have been poking her nose in his business and stumbled on some email exchanges between Jacques and myself. At the end of our conversation, before hanging up, she said: 'I hope you won't say anything to him. I'd very much like to keep this between the two of us.' I called Jacques right away and I said, I'm seeing your wife on Wednesday. Jacques already seemed to know about it. He sighed. The sigh of a coward, meaning, well, so be it. Couples disgust me. Their hypocrisy. Their smugness. Until that day, there was nothing I could do to resist Jacques Ecoupaud's appeal. A serial womaniser. My match in a man. Except that he is a secretary of state (he's always said *minister*). With all the trappings that go with it. Car with tinted windows, chauffeur, bodyguard. He can always get a restaurant table. Whereas I started out from nothing. I haven't even got my baccalaureate. I climbed the slope without anybody's help. Today, I'm an event decorator. I've made my name, I work with people in film and politics. I had dressed a function room in Bercy for a 'National

Seminar on the Achievements of Self-Employed Entrepreneurs' (I can still remember the title; we had stuck flags into the flowers). It was there that I met Jacques. The Minister for Tourism and Craft Industries. A pathetic brief, if you stop to think about it. The sort of no-neck, heavyset man who walks in and scans the room to check he's grabbed everybody's attention. The place was heaving with provincial entrepreneurs, who had come like lords to Paris with their wives dressed up to the nines. During the event, the vice president of some guild made a speech. Jacques Ecoupaud came over to me, I was at the back, close to a window, and he said to me, you see the guy who's just spoken? I said, yes. – Have you seen his bow tie? – Yes. – It's a bit thick, isn't it? Yes it is, I said. It's wooden, said Jacques Ecoupaud. – Wooden? The man's a craftsman, he makes timber frames. He's made a dicky bow out of wood, and he polishes it up with Pledge, said Jacques. I laughed and Jacques laughed his laugh, half seductive, half election campaign. And that one with the James Bond velvet briefcase? D'you know what he's called? Frank Ravioli. And he sells dry dog food. The next day, Jacques parked his Citroën C5 below my place and we spent the first part of the night together. Generally speaking, when it comes to men, I'm the one who takes the lead. I turn them on, I wrap them round my little finger, and then I clear off at first light. Sometimes I let myself join in the game. I get a bit attached. It lasts as long as it lasts. Until I get bored. Jacques Ecoupaud cut the ground from under my feet. Even today I can't figure out how I became so dependent on him. A no-neck guy who comes up to my shoulder. A middle-of-the-road smooth-talker. From the outset he tried to make out he was some great libertine. Along the lines of, I'm going to get down and dirty with you, little girl. He's always called me *little girl*. I'm fifty-six, nearly five foot eight, with a bust like Anita Ekberg, I found it touching to be called *little girl*. It's silly. A big libertine, who's he kidding? I still don't know what that means. But I was open to new experiences. One evening, he came over with a woman. A brunette of about forty who worked in social housing. She was called Corinne. I poured them an aperitif. Jacques took off his jacket and tie, and flopped on the sofa. The woman and I stayed in our chairs talking about the weather and the neighbourhood. Jacques said, sweethearts, make yourselves comfortable. We undressed a bit but not entirely.

Corinne seemed an old hand at this kind of situation. The dispassionate type who does what you tell her to. She undid her bra and hung it off a potted chrysanthemum. Jacques laughed. We were both wearing the same sort of lingerie designed to wake the dead. Then Jacques opened both arms equally wide and said, come here! We went and put ourselves on either side of him and he closed his arms again. We stayed like that for a while, giggling, playing with his big hairy belly, teasing his flies, when all of a sudden he said, so girlies, why don't you get to know each other? I'm still ashamed of those words. Ashamed of our position, of the harsh lighting, of Jacques' complete lack of imagination and his inability to dominate. I'd been expecting the Marquis de Sade but I got a guy who slouched and said *so girlies, why don't you get to know each other?* At the time, I chose to forget about it. If men only wanted to acknowledge one quality in us, this would be it. We give them a new lease. We reinstate them as soon as we can. We don't want to know that the chauffeur is an ex-customs officer, or the bodyguard a local security bumpkin from the Cantal. That the Citroën C5 is the lousiest of ministerial cars. That the big libertine has come to get down and dirty without even bringing a bottle of champagne. Thérèse Ecoupaud (that's the name of Jacques' wife) set our meeting for a café at Trinité. She said, I'll have a beige jacket and I'll be reading *Le Monde*. It sounded like a laugh a minute. I booked a manicure and a hair-colour appointment for the day before. The colourist made me a more golden blonde than usual. I spent an hour choosing my outfit. A red skirt, with a green round-neck sweater. Gigi Dool heels. And for the finishing touch, a natty off-white English-style trenchcoat. She was there. I spotted her straight away. From the street, behind the window. My age, but she looked ten years older. Make-up hastily applied. Short hair badly cut with visible roots. Blue scarf over a loose beige jacket. Right there and then I thought, it's over. Jacques Ecoupaud, it's over. I almost didn't go into the café. The sight of that legitimate and neglected woman was more of a killer than all the disappointments, the waiting, the unkept promises, the plates and candles laid out for nobody. She was sitting just inside from the terrace, not set back at all, glasses on the end of her nose, absorbed in her newspaper. A Latin teacher expecting her pupil. Thérèse Ecoupaud hadn't made the slightest effort before meeting her husband's mistress. What man can live with a woman like that? Couples disgust me. Their shrivelledness, their dusty complicity. There's nothing I like about this desultory structure that moves through time wearing the beard of isolation. I despise both parties and aspire only to destroy them. Still, I went inside. I held out my hand. I said, Chantal Audouin. She said, Thérèse Ecoupaud. I ordered a Bellini to piss her off. I unbuttoned my overcoat, without removing it, like a woman who can only allocate a small amount of time. She instantly made it clear that her attitude was nothing if not indifferent. Barely a glance. A careful turning of the coffee spoon held between her thumb and index finger. She said, my dear, my husband writes you emails. You reply. He makes declarations to you. Your response is passionate. When you become distressed, he apologises. He comforts you. You forgive him. Et cetera. The trouble with this correspondence, my dear, is that you believe it to be unique. You have painted a picture with yourself on one side, the warrior's haven, and on the other, the tedious wife and his national calling. It never occurred to you that other liaisons might be taking place at the same time. You thought you were the only one to whom my husband pours out his

125

soul, or sends messages, for example, at two o'clock in the morning, referring to himself as Jacquot (but these are silly details), 'Poor Jacquot, all alone in his room at Montauban, missing your skin, your lips and . . .' but you know the rest. It's identical for all three recipients. Three of you were sent the same message that night. More eager to please than the others, you replied warmly and, how can I put it, innocently. I wanted to meet you because I felt you were particularly smitten with my husband, said Thérèse Ecoupaud. I thought you might be glad to know so as not to fall from too great a height, said this ghastly woman. I said to Doctor Lorrain, doesn't it seem logical, Doctor, to try killing oneself after a meeting like that? The ideal would have been to kill the man, of course. I applaud those women who slaughter their lover, but not everybody's got the temperament. Doctor Lorrain asked me how I perceived Jacques Ecoupaud now that I was feeling better. I said, a sad little man. He raised his arms in his white coat and repeated after me as if I had just found the way to pastures new, a sad little man! – Yes, Doctor, a sad little man. But sad little men can dupe foolish women as you know. And what good is it to me to see him now as a sad little man? This sad little man degrades me and does me no good at all. Who says the heart grows lighter when faced with reality? Igor Lorrain nodded like a man who pretends to understand everything, and wrote I've no idea what assessment on my file. Leaving his consulting room, on the stairs of the mental health clinic, I ran into my favourite patient. A lanky, dark-haired young man with handsome pale eyes, always smiling. From Quebec. He said, hello, Chantal. I said, hello, Céline. I'd told him I was called Chantal and he'd told me he was called Céline. I think he reckons he's the singer Céline Dion. But maybe he's joking. He's always got a scarf around his neck. You can see him wandering along the corridors, or the garden pathways in good weather. He moves his lips and utters words you can't quite catch. He doesn't look at people on a level with them. It's as if he's addressing a distant fleet, as if he's praying from the top of a rock in order to attract those who are coming from afar, like in the myths.

Jean Erhenfried

Darius sat down on the huge orthopaedic chair, where nobody can be comfortable for my money. He sat down, wedged against its back like a man defeated. Anybody popping their head round the door would have been hard pressed to say which of us, he in that posture, or I, lying here with my dressings and drip, was the sorriest sight. I waited for him to speak. After a while, he said, with his neck thrust forward by the plump headrest: Anita's left me. Even though I was lying down in my hospital bed, I felt higher up than him. For Darius to say this with a crestfallen expression seemed to me bordering on the comical. All the more so when he added, in a voice that was barely audible, she's gone off with the landscape gardener. – The landscape gardener? – Yes. The guy who's been designing the shitty garden at Gassin for three years now. And who is ruining me with sub-Saharan plants that give me the creeps. I first met Darius, long before he was barred, at the Third Circle, one of those private members' clubs where shady deals are struck by left- and right-leaning oligarchs alike, steeped in political correctness and devout allegiance to the power of money. At the time, he was running several companies, including an engineering consultancy, if my memory serves me correctly. I had just left the international division of Safranz-Ulm Electric to be appointed chair of the board of directors. I grew fond of this boy nearly twenty-five years my junior, with his oriental charm. He had married Anita, the daughter of an English aristocrat, with whom he'd had two children who were, broadly speaking, flops. Darius Ardashir was shrewd as they come. He wormed his way through the system of leg-ups, back-scratching and pawns on the boards of directors, with a disarmingly casual approach. Never in a hurry, never cross. And the same with women. He ended up making his fortune as an intermediary in international deals. He got caught up in a few corruption cases, including one that was rather prickly involving the sale of a border surveillance system to Nigeria, and which, incidentally, warranted his expulsion from the Third Circle (for my money, a club that sends its rogues packing is a bloody awful club). Some of his associates did a stint in prison but he emerged relatively unscathed. I've always known him both as somebody who bounces back and as a loyal friend. When I was attacked by this filthy cancer, Darius behaved like a son. Before embarking on our conversation in earnest, I pressed all sorts of buttons in an attempt to raise the upper part of my bed. Darius watched my efforts, and the resulting series of absurd positions, glassy-eyed, unmoving. A nurse appeared, presumably because I'd rung for her. – What are you trying to do, Monsieur Erhenfried? – Sit up! – Doctor Chemla will be along in a minute. He knows you haven't got a temperature any more. – Tell him I've had enough and he's to let me out tomorrow. She fixed up my bed and tucked me in like a child. I asked Darius whether he wanted something to drink. He declined and the girl left. Right, I said. This landscape gardener, it's not just a passing crush? – She wants a divorce. I paused before saying, you never set great store by Anita. He gave me a stunned look, as if I was talking complete and utter nonsense. – She's had the best life in the world. I understand that, I said. – I gave her everything. Name me anything she hasn't had. Houses, jewels, staff. Extravagant trips abroad. She'll get nothing from me, Jean. All my assets are tied up in the company. The villa at Gassin, rue de la Tour, the furniture, the artworks, nothing's in my name. They can starve. – You were unfaithful to her. – What's that got to do with it? – You can't begrudge her taking a lover. – Women don't take lovers. They become infatuated, they make a song and dance. They go stark raving mad. A man needs a safe place from which to face the world. You can't spread your wings if you haven't got a fixed point, a base camp. Anita is the house. She is the family. It doesn't matter where you work up your appetite, provided you eat at home. I don't get attached to women. The only one that counts is the next one. The stupid bitch goes and sleeps with the gardener and wants to run off with him. Where's the sense in that? While I was listening to Darius, I could see the drops from the drip falling one by one.

They looked strangely irregular, I was on the verge of calling the nurse back. I said, would you have agreed to her living like you? – Meaning? – That she could have inconsequential affairs? He shook his head. He took a white handkerchief out of his pocket and carefully unfolded it before blowing his nose. I reflected such a gesture could only belong to a singular kind of man. He said, no. Because it's not her style. And then he said glumly, I was in London these last two days (an important trip which she completely ruined for me), and on the return journey the Eurostar stopped for a few minutes at the top of France, in some outlying area. Just in front of my window there was a small, red-brick suburban house, with red tiles and a tidy picket fence. Geraniums at the windows. And, attached to the walls, in hanging pots, there were still some flowers in bloom. Do you know what I thought, Jean? I thought, in this house, somebody has decided to be happy. I assumed he was going to carry on but he fell quiet. He stared at the floor. I said to myself, he's come to the end of the road. When somebody like Darius Ardashir goes looking for happiness in imitation brickwork and macramé flowerpot holders it's a sure sign of collapse. And more worryingly as far as he's concerned, I thought, when he views happiness as the aim. As for me, I urgently needed to summon a medical professional because the plastic tube was pumping air bubbles towards my arm. Do you know how old Anita is? asked Darius. – Are those bubbles normal? – What bubbles? Those are drops. It's the medicine. – You think so? Look more closely. He got out his glasses and stood up to take a closer look at the drip. – Drops. – Are you sure? Tap the pouch. – What for? – Tap it. Tap it. It helps. Darius tapped the pouch of serum and went to sit back down again. I said, I can't see anything any more. I've had enough of all this plumbing. – Do you know how old Anita is? – Tell me. – Forty-nine. Is that any kind of an age to develop ambitions for blossoming, for finding passionate love and that kind of rubbish? You see, Jean, I often think of Dina. You had a wife who understood life. Dina is in the sky now. You Jews haven't got heaven, what have you got? – We don't have anything. – Well, she's in a good place, that's for sure. She left you with your sons, they're nice, they look after you, your daughter as well, your son-in-law, your grandchildren. She knew how to create a family environment. As we grow old, it matters, having a hand to grab hold of. I'll end up like a rat. Anita will tell you I've got my just deserts. Which is a stupid expression. What's that got to do with it? I've provided a sumptuous apartment, sumptuous properties, what do they all think, that it falls out of the sky? Why am I killing myself, I leave at eight in the morning, I get to bed at midnight, doesn't she understand that it's for her? And the boys, those two dead losses who'll squander everything, don't they understand that it's for them? No. Criticisms, criticisms, criticisms. And a romance with a joker who plants frangipani trees. I'd rather she left me for a woman. I asked, are you comfortable in that chair? – Very comfortable. The day before, Ernest had tried it for less than a minute before opting for the folding chair. Listening to Darius, I recalled an afternoon Dina and I had spent at the house doing some clearing out. We had rediscovered a pile of old-fashioned hand-embroidered linen that came from her mother, and a handsome set of tableware from Italy. We had wondered, what's the point in any of this now? Dina had spread the tablecloth over a sofa. Well–ironed, yellowing somewhat. She had lined up the inlaid porcelain cups. Objects that have a value one day become useless burdens over time. I didn't know what to say to Darius. A couple is the most unfathomable thing. You never understand a couple, not even when you're part of it. Doctor Chemla walked into the room. Smiling, affable as ever. I was glad he had come because my arm was starting to turn gangrenous. I made the introductions, Darius Ardashir, a dear friend, Doctor Philip Chemla, my saviour. And I immediately added, Doctor, doesn't my arm look swollen to you? I think the drip is missing the vein. Chemla pressed down on my fingers and on my forearm. He looked at my wrist, turned the valve to adjust the flow and said, we'll finish this pouch and then we're done. Tomorrow you'll be home again. I'll come back to see you this evening, we'll take a little stroll down the corridor. When he had gone, Darius said, what exactly did you have? – A urinary infection. – How old's your doc? – Thirty-six. – Too young. – A genius. – Too young. I said, what are you going to do? He leaned forward, held out his arms like a man lifting the void, and let them fall back down again. I saw his gaze stray to my bedside table. He said, what are you reading? – *The Destruction of the*

136

European Jews by Raul Hilberg. – Is that all you could find for hospital? – It's perfect for hospital. When things are hard, you should read sad books. Darius picked up the book, which is hefty. He leafed through it, glassy-eyed again. – So you'd recommend it. – Very much so. He did at least smile. He put the book down and he said, she should have given me some warning. I can't come to terms with her betraying me in secret. Despite Chemla checking, it still looked to me as though my arm was swelling up. I said, take a look at both my arms, do they seem the same thickness to you? Darius stood up, he put his glasses back on, looked at my arms and said, exactly the same. Then he sat down again. We remained in silence for a short while, listening to the sounds in the corridor, the trolleys, the voices. Then Darius said, women have hijacked the role of martyrs. They've theorised about it out loud. They moan and want to be pitied. But in reality the true martyr is the man. Hearing this reminded me of what my friend Serge had said, in the early stages of his Alzheimer's. He wanted, I don't know why, to get to rue de l'Homme-Marié. Nobody knew where this street of the Married Man was. In the end we understood that he was talking about rue des Martyrs. I told this anecdote to Darius, who vaguely recollected hearing it before. He asked me, how's he doing? I said, not too bad. The main thing is not to contradict him, I always let him be right. Darius nodded. He stared at a patch of floor over by the door and said, it's a marvellous disease.

Damien Barnèche

My dad used to say, if somebody asks what your dad does, just say consultant. In reality, he received a consultant's payslip in exchange for a bridge partnership with a guy who dealt in market concessions. My grandad lost all his money at the races and my dad was voluntarily barred from the casinos for years. Loula listens to me like the stuff I'm telling her is unbelievable. She's dead cute. Every morning she sits in my car, I mean in the car provided by the film production company so I can pick her up and drop her off. She sits in front, next to me, a bit sleepy. My instructions are not to talk to her unless she says something to me, I'm supposed to respect how tired she is or if she needs to concentrate. But Loula Moreno asks me questions, takes an interest in me, she doesn't just talk about herself like most actresses. I tell her I'm into film, that I work in production but I'd rather be in the director's chair. To be honest I don't really know what I want to do. I'm the first Barnèche who's not a gambler. She calls me Damien and I call her Madame Moreno as a mark of respect, even though I'm twenty-two and she's only just turned thirty (she told me). As the days have gone by, I've been telling her about my life. Loula Moreno is inquisitive and sharp. She soon noticed I was interested in Géraldine, the assistant dresser, a tiny brunette with pale eyes and hair all over the place. My first impressions were mixed because we were talking music and I found out right away that she liked the Black Eyed Peas and the singer Zaz. Normally, I'd stop right there. But maybe us being in Klosterneuburg (we started filming in Austria) made me more tolerant, or more slack. Especially since we found out right away that we're both crazy about Pim's biscuits. We remembered that when we were little, they used to make a white-chocolate-and-cherry Pim's. We both agreed about the Casino supermarket own brand not being as good. Géraldine asked me if I thought that one day Pim's would make a caramel Pim's. I said, yes, as long as they made the biscuit harder or else the caramel had to be very light because you can't have runny on floppy. Géraldine said, but then it wouldn't be a Pim's. I couldn't have agreed more. She didn't know pear Pim's which are very rare and not many people know about them. I said to her, they're as good as it gets with Pim's. The jam is quite thick, compared to the raspberry or orange ones, but you wouldn't know until you take a bite. Then it spreads. The orange hits you straight away, but the pear takes its time. It melts into the sponge. Even the presentation is perfect. Classy packaging. Not some lousy green, they've used a sort of fawn colour, you see. She was all fired up. At the end I said, when it comes to your first pear Pim's, you should eat it staring at the packet. She said, yes, yes, of course! I fell in love with her because it's so rare for a girl to understand that kind of thing. Loula approves. I can't work out if I stand a chance with Géraldine. When I'm really attracted to a girl, I'm not the kind of guy who just goes for it. I need a sort of safeguard. In Klosterneuburg, I got the feeling she liked me. Since we've been back, she's been trying it on with the boom-operator. A giant shrimp who says hello with a scout's salute (I'm not sure it's meant to be funny, and if it is meant to be funny, that's even worse). And there's another problem, which didn't exist in Austria: she wears ballerina pumps. Even with dresses. At uni, when you bent down you saw a forest of legs in ballerina pumps. For me, ballerina pumps equal boredom and no sex. Loula asked me to make a list of all the things that irritate me in a girl. I said it went up to a number just below infinity. – Go on. I said, if a girl has a silly haircut. If she analyses everything. If she's a good Catholic girl. If she's an activist. If she's only friends with girls. If she likes Justin Timberlake. If she has a blog. Loula laughed. I said, if she can't laugh the way you do. One evening, there was a small party to mark one of the cast member's last day of filming. Loula advised me not to let the boom-operator gain ground. I found myself sitting, shoulders touching, with Géraldine, in the stairwell leading down to the basement where the scenery is stored. I'd swiped a bottle of red wine, we were drinking out of plastic glasses. Especially me. I said (in that gravelly voice that actors in American series use for the pre-fuck scene), if I was president, there's a number of reforms I'd put through straight away. A European directive against coat hangers that claim to hold your trousers but drop them as soon as your back's turned. A law against tissue paper inside shoes (it's called tissue paper, but it's a cross between tissue paper and tracing paper), which just wastes your time and says 'I'm brand new'. A law to stop you being hassled by the leaflet when you open a box of medicine. You're fumbling around to find your sleeping pill and you land on a piece of paper, so you bin the leaflet because it pisses you off. We should charge laboratories with murder given the risk they make you take. Géraldine said, d'you take sleeping pills? – No, antihistamines. – What's that? I didn't have enough alcohol in my system not to see the scale of the problem. Not only was Géraldine not being charmed into my arms by my sweet nothings, but she didn't know the word *antihistamine*. And that's without mentioning the disapproving tone about sleeping pills, a sure sign of an inflexible personality and New Age leanings. I said, medicine for allergies. – You have an allergy? – Asthma. – Asthma? What was with her repeating everything? After a swig from the bottle I said dolefully, as well as hay fever, and other sorts of allergies. And then I kissed her. She let it happen. I pushed her back onto the stairs, against the concrete wall of the warehouse, and I started to grope her any old how. She was wriggling and saying something I couldn't understand which got on my nerves, and I said, what, as I was getting turned on by her, what? What are you saying? She repeated, not here, not here Damien! She was trying to push me off her, the way girls do, half yes, half no, I stuck my head under her T-shirt, she wasn't wearing a bra, I latched onto a nipple with my lips, I could hear incomprehensible groanings, I was stroking her thighs, her buttocks, I'd reached the top of her panties, I was trying to steer her hand onto my cock, and all of a sudden she reared up, she pushed me away with her arms, her legs, kicking in every direction and shouting, stop, stop! I ended up pinned to the opposite wall, staring at a girl who was bright red and outraged . . . She said, you're sick! I said, what did I do? – You're kidding me? – I'm sorry. I thought you . . . you didn't seem to mind it . . . – Not here. Not like that. – What d'you mean, not like that? – Not roughly like that. With no foreplay. A woman needs foreplay, did nobody tell you? She was trying to rearrange her hair, she repeated the same movement ten times to pull it all back. I thought, *foreplay*, what a dire word. I said, leave your hair alone, it's pretty when it's a mess. – But I don't want it to be a mess. I drank the dregs and I said, it's revolting this plonk. – Why are you drinking it? – Come and kiss me. – No. They'd put some music on upstairs, but I couldn't figure out what it was. I held out my hands entreatingly. – Come on. – No. She twisted her hair behind her head and stood up. I pressed my head against the wall and let my body slide down. She was standing there, arms dangling. Me, on the ground, crushing the plastic glass. So this was being young, having the years ahead of you. As in nothing. A big hole. But not a hole you fall into. It's up there, in front of you. My dad's right to live through cards. Géraldine came over and crouched down next to me. I was starting to get a headache. She said, you okay? – Yes. – What are you thinking about? – Nothing. – Go on, tell me. – Nothing, really. I waited 'til I was a bit calmer and then I kissed her without touching anything else. I stood up, I fixed my clothes and I said, I'm going home. She stood up again in a flash, she said, I'm going home too. Are you angry? – No. Switching like that does my head in. The soppy voice all of a sudden. I strode back up the stairs, I could feel her hurrying to keep up with me. Just before we got to the top, she said, Damien?

145

– What? – Nothing. Up on the ground floor, there was a nice vibe, people were dancing, Loula Moreno had left of course. The next day, in the car, I gave her the outline of the evening. Loula said, how did you leave each other? – I took the car and I went back home. – How did you say goodbye? – Bye, bye, a peck on the cheek. Rubbish, said Loula. Rubbish, I repeated. Day had hardly broken, it was foul weather. I'd switched on everything you can switch on in a car, windscreen wipers, defogger, heating on full. I said, in real life, I have a scooter. Loula nodded. – I was on roller skates when my mates were on bikes, on a bike when they were on scooters, and now I'm on a scooter when they're in cars. I'm the boy who always times it just right. I said, there's a well-known recipe to taking down the ladies, everybody knows it, and it involves not saying a word. The guys who appeal are the silent, moody types. But I don't think I'm good-looking enough, or naturally intriguing enough to keep quiet. I talk too much, I fool about, I want to be funny all the time. Even with you, I want to be funny. Often after a series of jokes, I go all moody because I'm kicking myself. Especially when they fall flat. I freeze up, and become gloomy for quarter of an hour. And then the cheerful me is

146

back again. It pisses me off, all this pussyfooting about to seduce somebody. Loula said, what kind of scooter do you have? – A Yamaha Xenter 125. D'you know about them? – For a while, I used to have a Vespa. Pink, like in *Roman Holiday*. I said, I can picture you on that. You must have looked really cute. Wasn't it in black and white, that film? She thought about it. She said, oh yes, so it was. But it looked pink. Maybe it wasn't pink after all.

Luc Condamine

Yesterday, I said, I thrashed Juliette with the dog lead. Have you got a dog? said Lionel. Robert was making us spaghetti in his kitchen. With Neapolitan *sugo*. That's how I like to see the two idiots. Over the kitchen table. Without the women. Left to our own devices and our own worst natures, as Lionel would say. I hit my daughter with the dog lead, I repeated. After a row over her insolence, just as she was leaving the room, I said, and don't slam the door! So she slammed the door extra hard. I picked up the lead that was lying around, I caught up with her in the corridor and I gave her a good hiding. I didn't feel any remorse or embarrassment. As a matter of fact I felt rather relieved.

That child imposes a reign of terror on our household and screeches at us non-stop. When she heard that I had hit our daughter with the dog lead, Anne-Laure pulled a pained face, without uttering a word. She adopts these Yiddish theatrical expressions to make her contempt known to me. It's recent. She left the room, returning a few minutes later, in the grand punitive silence of women, to show me the lacerations on the arm and one part of the back. I said, she deserved it. Juliette looked me up and down with her face that was all puffy and red and said, I hate you. I thought she looked rather sweet and her voice sounded normal enough. Anne-Laure said, you should see somebody. Perhaps I should see somebody. I'd forgotten you had a dog, said Lionel. – A long rat. Call that a dog? Top-notch this wine. Brunello di Montalcino 2006. Good call. I'm clean out of patience when it comes to women. The other day I had my mother on the telephone, Anne-Laure in front of the mirror (she thinks she's wrinkly), Juliette yelling at her sister, I said to myself, fuck me! I'm going to ask the newspaper to send me somewhere far away. What about Paola, quizzed Robert, are you still seeing her? – Still seeing her. But I'm going to stop. You haven't said anything to Odile? – No, no.

Why are you going to stop? – Because there comes a time when out of the courtesan bursts the real woman, warts and all. I only like the girls in seamen's bars, but I seem to attract the brainy type that invites me to poetry evenings. She deserves much better than you, said Robert. – That's my gripe. And while we're on the subject, Virginie Déruelle, what's happening there? Who's she? asked Lionel. A girl he met at his gym and now wants to pass on to me, answered Robert. – And did pass on. – If you like. – So, anyway? Robert laughed and pulled out a long piece of spaghetti. – Try it, cooked enough? Shall I leave it a bit longer? – It's good. Tell us! – No. Here we are ready to give him some invaluable advice on his affair, but he wants to keep it to himself, I said to Lionel. Just then, we heard music blaring from somewhere in the apartment. – What's that? It's Simon, he'll get us kicked out of this building, the little bastard, said Robert. He abandoned the pasta and ran down the corridor. The music stopped dead. We heard a torrent of words. He came back in with his younger son, who has such a likeable face. I wish I'd had a son. Robert said, if the neighbours ring, it's up to your brother to sort it out. And I'll be on their side one hundred per cent. What d'you want, some milk? Antoine mumbled, blackcurrant juice. – Not at night, not after brushing your teeth. Blackcurrant juice, repeated Antoine. – Why don't you want some milk? You love milk! – I want blackcurrant juice. What the hell, give him some blackcurrant juice, I said. Robert poured him a glass of blackcurrant juice. Off you go, badger, bed. Robert drained the spaghetti and tipped it into a dish on the table. Lionel said, we had that for years with Jacob. The neighbours spent their lives knocking and ringing. What news of Jacob? Is he still doing his internship in London? questioned Robert. Lionel nodded. What kind of internship? I asked. – At a record label. – Which one? – A small label. – Is he happy with it? – Seems to be. Robert was bustling about serving us. He grated the Parmesan. He chopped the basil, which he scattered over the *sugo*. He laid out the condiments, Sicilian olive oil, and a chilli oil. He filled our glasses. It was nice, just the three of us. I said, it's nice, just the three of us. We clinked our glasses. To friendship. To old age. To the quality of our future nursing homes. And to the rare honour of Lionel's company, said Robert. Lionel tried objecting. He's right, I said, admit you're never free. It's easier to get an appointment with Nelson Mandela than it is with Lionel Hutner. Hey! Just a little joke, my friend! You're the only who's happy in your relationship. That's bound to keep you busy. The door opened to reveal Simon, Odile and Robert's eldest. A child's body and a lock of wavy brown hair, mysteriously sticky, pulled down over his forehead, betraying a certain fashion awareness. What now? said Robert. We don't want to be disturbed any more if it's all the same to you. – Is there any blackcurrant juice left? Oh great, pasta, can I try some? – Put a little on a plate and make yourself scarce. I watched the thrill and excitement in the eyes of this boy wearing red pyjamas that were too short for him, as the spaghetti, tomato sauce and Parmesan formed a small heap on his plate. I waited for him to leave with his blackcurrant juice in the other hand, and I said, being happy is a predisposition. You can't be happy in love if you're not predisposed to being happy. Now look, old boy, you'll end up putting a downer on the evening, said Robert. Concentrate on your pasta. No compliments? Terrific, said Lionel. – When we die, Anne-Laure and I, the final reckoning will be apocalyptic. But who cares about the final reckoning? If it turns out I've wasted my life, I couldn't care less. I'm thinking of taking up judo in September. I'd like some pasta too, said Antoine, who had just reappeared. You've already eaten, you two are a pain in the neck, go back to bed, bellowed Robert. How come Simon gets to eat again? – Because he's twelve. That's really going to convince him, I intervened. Robert grabbed a plate and threw a handful of spaghetti onto it. No sauce, just Parmesan, said Antoine. – Go on, clear off. Robert uncorked another bottle of Brunello. We're not hearing much from you, I said to Lionel. Lionel looked odd. He was staring at the bottom of his glass as he turned it. Then he announced, in a hollow voice, Jacob has been sectioned. A silence followed. He said, he's not in London, he's in a mental health clinic at Rueil-Malmaison. Can I count on your complete discretion? Not a word to Anne-Laure, to Odile or to anybody else. We said, of course, Robert and me. Of course. Robert filled Lionel's glass. Lionel drank several mouthfuls in a row. – You remember his propensity for . . . his infatuation with . . . with Céline Dion? As soon as he said the name, Lionel started laughing and spluttering, uncontrollably, his eyes misty and bloodshot and his body racked by spasms. We were transfixed, seeing him laugh like that. He tried to say something else, but it was as if he could only repeat the name, and even then not all of it, in a strangled voice, each time drowned by tragic mirth. He was wiping away the tears on his cheeks with the palm of his hand, it was hard to tell where they came from laughter or crying. After a while, he calmed down. Robert patted his shoulder. We stayed there. All three of us round the table. Without understanding and without knowing what to do. Then Lionel stood up. He ran the cold water in the sink and splashed his face several times. He turned towards us and said, making a visible effort to master his voice, Jacob takes himself for Céline Dion. He is convinced that he *is* Céline Dion. I didn't dare look at Robert. Lionel had uttered the second sentence with extreme gravitas and was staring at us with terror in his eyes. I thought, as long as I don't look at Robert, I can maintain an expression of friendly concern. As long as I take no notice of Robert, I can maintain the painful mask that Lionel needs. He was the most joyous child on earth, said Lionel. The most inventive. He used to create whole landscapes in his bedroom, archipelagos, a zoo, a car park. He would organise all sorts of shows. Not just musical ones. He had a shop with toy money. He would call out, the shop's open! I don't know why, but evoking the shop plunged Lionel into an anxious reverie. He stared at a fixed point on the tiling. Then he said, you're right, being happy is a predisposition. Perhaps we shouldn't be happy in childhood. I've asked myself the question. Perhaps being happy in childhood doesn't serve you well in later life. Seeing Lionel standing in the middle of the kitchen, with his trousers hitched too high, his shirt badly tucked in, I thought how little it takes for a man to look vulnerable. Behind me Robert said, come and sit back down again, old boy. I made the mistake of turning round. One second was all it took for our eyes to meet. I couldn't say which of us cracked first. We hunched over the table, choking with laughter. I remember gripping Robert's arm to beg him to stop, I can still hear the sound of his uncontrolled snorting. We got up, still laughing, we begged Lionel to forgive us. Robert put his arms round Lionel, I joined in, and we hugged him like two shamefaced children hiding in their mother's skirt. Then Robert pulled away. By dint of what I presume was intense concentration, he had managed to recompose a serious face. He said, you know we're not laughing *at* you. Lionel was munificent, smiling gently, he said, I know, I know. We sat back down at the table. Robert filled our glasses. We clinked them again. To friendship. To Jacob's health. We asked a few questions. Lionel said, I'm in awe of Pascaline. I know she's worried sick but she stays cheerful, she keeps positive. Don't tell her that you know. If she talks to you about it one day, you know nothing. We promised not to say anything. We tried to talk about something else. Lionel got me going on my recent reporting. I told them about the inauguration of the Jewish Memorial in Skopje. An open-air ceremony on plastic chairs. The strains of the brass band rising from a way off, tinny as a toy. The three Macedonian soldiers, like skinheads in cloaks, their arms horizontal, bearing the cushion with a can of soda water which in reality was an urn containing the ashes of the victims of Treblinka. The whole thing completely grotesque. A month later, another brass band in Rwanda. The eighteenth anniversary of the genocide in the stadium in Kigali. Surging through a gate like the lions entering in *Ben-Hur*, these guys goose-stepping, twirling batons. I said, why do all these massacres end with such fanfare? You've got a point, remarked Lionel. And we started laughing, all three of us, probably drunkenly.

Hélène Barnèche

The other day, on the bus, a portly man sat down opposite
me, in the window seat. It was a while before I took any
interest in him. I only looked up because I could feel his
eyes resting on me. He was examining me from head to toe,
with a very serious look, as if divining something. I did what
you do in that situation, you hold the other person's gaze to
register your indifference before returning to your thoughts.
But I felt uncomfortable. I could sense that his interest
wasn't waning and I wondered if I shouldn't say something.
I was considering this when I heard, Hélène? Hélène
Barnèche? I said, do we know each other? He said, as if he
was the only one in the world, and so he was, Igor. It was

less the name than his way of pronouncing it that I recognised in a flash. Lingering on the *o*, slipping a pretentious irony into those two syllables. I repeated the name, dumbly, and it was my turn to take a good look at his face. I am a woman who doesn't like photos (I never take them myself), who doesn't like any image, happy or sad, that might reawaken an emotion. Emotions are scary. I want life to keep moving forward and for everything to be erased over time. I couldn't connect this new Igor with the one from the past. Neither his build nor a single one of his magical qualities. But I remembered the stretch of time that had carried his name. When I knew Igor Lorrain, I was twenty-six, and he was hardly older. I was already married to Raoul and working at the Caisse des Depôts as a secretary. Igor was studying medicine. At the time, Raoul spent his nights in the cafés playing cards. A friend, Yorgos, had brought Igor along to the Darcey, on place Clichy. I was there nearly every evening but I always used to head home for my early night. Igor offered to give me a lift. He had a blue 2CV, which started up with a crank under the bonnet because the radiator grille was dented. He was tall and slim. He was wavering between bridge and psychiatry. Most of all he was crazy. It was hard to resist him. One evening, he leaned towards me at a red light and he said, my poor Hélène, you really have been deserted. And he kissed me. It wasn't true, I didn't feel deserted, but by the time I'd asked myself the question I was already in his arms. We hadn't eaten, he took me to a little bistro at Porte de Saint-Cloud. I instantly understood who I was dealing with. He ordered two plates of chicken with green beans. When the food arrived, he tasted it and he said, it needs salt. I said, no, this is fine for me. He said, no, it's not salty enough, add some salt. I said, it's really fine like this, Igor. He said, add some salt, I'm telling you. And I added some salt. Igor Lorrain came from the north, like me. He was from Béthune. His father worked in river transport. It wasn't a barrel of laughs at my house. Even less so at his. In our families, if you weren't being given a walloping, you were being punched or having an object hurled at your face. For a long time I fought over the slightest thing. I hit the other girls, I hit my boyfriends. I hit Raoul to begin with, but he just laughed. I didn't know what else to do when he made me cross. I beat him. He would make a show of bending double like he was being attacked by one of the plagues of Egypt, or else he would laugh and grab both my wrists with one hand. I've never hit Damien. I haven't hit anybody since I had my son. On the number 95 bus, which goes from place Clichy to the Porte de Vanves, I remembered what had chained me to Igor Lorrain. Not love, or whatever name you give to that feeling, but brutality. He leaned forward and he said, do you recognise me? I said, yes and no. He smiled. And I also remembered how in the past I could never give him a straight answer. – Is your name still Hélène Barnèche ? – Yes. – Are you still married to Raoul Barnèche? – Yes. I didn't want to be monosyllabic, but I couldn't bring myself to address him with any familiarity. He had long salt-and-pepper hair, strangely pulled back, and a fleshy neck. I rediscovered in his eyes the dark wild streak that had drawn me in. I ticked off everything in my head. My hairstyle, my dress and jacket, my hands. He leaned closer to say, are you happy? I said, yes, and I thought, what a nerve. He nodded and tried to look touched, you're happy, congratulations. I wanted to slap him. Thirty years of harmonious living brushed away in ten seconds. I said, and what about you, Igor? He made himself more comfortable on the seat, and replied, me, no. – Are you a psychiatrist? – Psychiatrist and psychoanalyst. I pulled a face indicating that these subtleties were lost on me. He waved a hand indicating that it didn't matter. He said, where are you going? Those four words turned everything upside down for me. *Where are you going*, as if we had seen one another the day before. With the same tone he had used in the past, as if we had done nothing with our lives apart from marking time. *Where are you going* cut me to the quick. I felt conflicting emotions welling up. There is an abandoned part of me that aspires to being tyrannised. Raoul has never *controlled* me. My Rouli has only ever thought about playing and his own enjoyment. It's never crossed his mind to keep an eye on his feisty little wife. Igor Lorrain wanted to bind me hand and foot. He wanted to know in detail where I was going, what I was doing and with whom. He used to say, you belong to me. I would say, no. He would squeeze my neck, he would squeeze hard until I said, I belong to you. There were other times when he would hit me. I had to repeat it because my words failed to reach him. I would struggle, I would lash out, but he always overcame me. We would end up in bed to console one another. Then I would escape. He lived in a tiny maid's room on boulevard Exelmans. I would escape down the stairs. He would call out over the handrail, say that you belong to me, and I would say as I was hurtling down, no, no, no. He would catch up with me, pin me against the wall or the lift cage (sometimes the neighbours would go past), and he would say, where are you going, you little slut, you know you belong to me. We would make love again on the steps. A woman wants to be dominated. A woman wants to be put in chains. It's not something you can explain to everybody. I was trying to resurrect the man sitting opposite me on the bus. His good looks now old and worn out. I didn't recognise the movement of his body. But his gaze, yes. His voice too. – Where are you going? – To Pasteur. – To do what at Pasteur? – That's out of order. – Do you have children? – A son. – How old is he? – Twenty-two. How about you, do you have children? – What's he called? – My son? Damien. How about you, do you have children? Igor Lorrain shrugged. He stared out of the window at an advert for domestic central heating. Was he capable of having children? Clearly. Anybody can have children. I'd like to have known with what kind of woman. I wanted to ask him if he was married, but I didn't. I felt sorry for him, and for me. Two people approaching old age, being carted around Paris, weighted down by their lives. He had placed a battered leather briefcase, like a satchel, next to him. The handle was discoloured. He seemed very alone to me. His bearing, his clothing. It's plain when there's nobody taking care of you. Maybe he's got somebody, but not somebody who takes care of him. I pamper my Rouli. You could even say I go over the top. I choose his clothes, I dye his eyebrows, I stop him from drinking, or eating the bowl of nibbles. In my own way, I am also alone. Raoul is sweet and affectionate (except when we're bridge partners, then he changes into somebody else), but I know he gets bored in my company (except when we go to the cinema). He's happy with his pals, he has invented an existence for himself outside of real life and drudgery. My friend Chantal says that Raoul reminds her of politicians. People who are always absent even when they're there. Damien has left home. I made myself push him out a bit. When I was tidying up his bedroom afterwards, I found relics from every stage of his life. One evening, I sat on his bed and I cried when I opened a box full of painted chestnuts. Children leave, and so they should, it's normal. Igor Lorrain said, I'm getting off here, come with me. I looked to see the stop, it was Rennes–Saint-Placide. I said, I'm getting off at Pasteur–Docteur-Roux. He shrugged as if that was the last destination on earth. He stood up. He said, come on, Hélène. *Come on, Hélène.* And he held out his hand. I thought, this is crazy. I thought, we're still alive. I put my hand on top of his. He pulled me past the other passengers towards the exit and we got off the bus. It was a fine day. There were roadworks. We sneaked into a maze of breeze blocks and hoardings to cross the rue de Rennes. People were walking in both directions and jostling one another. There was noise everywhere. Igor held my hand tightly. We came out onto boulevard Raspail. I was infinitely grateful to him for not letting go. The sun was blinding me. I could just make out, as if for the first time, the rows of trees in the middle, the clumps of plants in their blue-green wrought-iron enclosure. I had no idea where we were going. Did he know? One day Igor Lorrain had said to me, it was a mistake to put me in a human society. God should have put me in the savannah and made me a tiger. I would have ruled over my territory, giving no quarter. We were heading back up towards Denfert. He said to me, you're still just a slip of a thing. He was as tall as before, but more thickset. I had to run a little to keep up with him.

Jeannette Blot

I look hideous, hideous, hideous. I don't even want to come out of the changing cubicle to show Marguerite. I can't wear tailored clothes. I don't have a waist any more. My chest has grown bigger. I can't wear anything low cut. Once upon a time, yes. Today, no. Marguerite isn't being realistic. And anyway you'll never see her without a crew neck or a little scarf. My daughter and my sister-in-law have got it into their heads that they need to change my wardrobe for I don't know what psychological reasons. When we celebrated my seventieth birthday the other evening, Odile said to me, you don't wear clothes, Mummy, you cover yourself in fabric. – So what? Who's looking at me?

Certainly not Ernest. Your father doesn't even know I have a body any more. The next day, she called me to say that as she was passing Franck et Fils, she had seen a little brown dress with an orange trim. It would look perfect on you, Mummy, she said. I'll grant you that on the model in the department store window it had a certain attraction. Does it suit you? asks Marguerite from behind the curtain. – No, no, not at all! – Show me. – No, no, it's not worth it! I try to take off the dress. The zip gets stuck. I'm close to tearing the whole thing to shreds. I come out of the cubicle which is a suffocating coffin, help me take it off, Marguerite! – Let me see you! You look great! What don't you like? – I don't like anything. It's all horrible. Are you nearly there? – And what about the blouse? – I hate frills. – There aren't any. – Yes, there are. – Why are you so uptight, Jeannette? – Because you and Odile are forcing me to do something unnatural. Going shopping like this is excruciating. – The zip is caught in the lining. Don't wriggle about like that. I start to cry. Marguerite is busying herself behind me. I don't want her to notice. It's ridiculous. You hold back the tears for years only to find yourself crying for no reason in a dressing room at Franck et Fils. Are you okay? says

Marguerite. She's got sharp hearing. She annoys me, the way she notices everything. In the end, I prefer people who don't notice anything at all. You learn to be alone. You don't have to explain yourself. Marguerite says, don't move, I'm nearly there. In a book by Gilbert Cesbron, I think it is, a woman asks her confessor: should we succumb to grief, or should we fight against it and contain it? The confessor replies, holding back the tears doesn't help anybody. The grief remains lodged somewhere. There we go, crows Marguerite. I disappear back into the cubicle to liberate myself. I put my own clothes back on, I try to freshen up my face. The dress slips off the coat hanger and falls, I scoop it up and leave it like a rag on the stool. Out on the street, I urge Marguerite to abandon this project of making me stylish again. My sister-in-law keeps stopping in front of every window display. Clothing, shoes, leather goods and even household linen. It must be said that she lives in Rouen, poor thing. From time to time, she tries to egg me on, but it's clear that she's the one who wants to go inside, to touch the bag, to try something on. I say to her, that'd suit you. Let's go in and see. She replies, oh no, no, I've already got so much useless stuff, I don't know what to do with it any more. I press the point, that's a nice little jacket, it would go with everything. Marguerite shakes her head. I'm worried she's just trying to be tactful. This is depressing, two women walking past a row of fashion boutiques without wanting anything. I don't dare ask Marguerite whether she's got a man in her life (what a stupid expression, what does it mean to have a man in one's life? Look at me, with one on paper, but none in my life). When you've got a man in your life, you wonder about silly things, the quality of a lipstick, the shape of a bra, the colour of your hair. It fills your time. It's fun. Perhaps Marguerite has these sorts of preoccupations. I could ask her but I'm afraid of a revelation hurting me. It's been so many years since I aspired to any kind of transformation. When he was at the peak of his career, Ernest would check my appearance. There was nothing thoughtful about this. We went out a lot. I was part of the decorum. The other day, I took my grandson Simon to the Louvre to see the paintings of the Italian Renaissance. He lights up my days that little one. He's interested in art, aged twelve. Looking at those paintings with their characters in dark clothes hugging the walls, those cruel and wicked beings from ancient times, walking hunched over, on their way to who knows where, I thought, what has become of these evil spirits? Have they disappeared from all the books, disappeared with impunity? My thoughts turned to Ernest. Ernest Blot, my husband, is the same as those evening shadows. Deceitful, lying, without pity. There must be something twisted in me to have wished to be loved by this man. Women are attracted to appalling men, because appalling men appear masked at the ball. They arrive with mandolins and fancy-dress costumes. I was pretty. Ernest was possessive, I mistook jealousy for love. I've let forty-eight years go by. We live with the illusion of repetition, like the sun rising and setting. We rise and we go to bed, in the belief that we're repeating ourselves, but that's not the case. Marguerite and her brother are not alike. She is friendly, she has scruples. She says, Jeannette, do you still want to have a go at driving? I say, what d'you think? You don't think it's madness? We start laughing. All of a sudden we're excited. It's been thirty years since I took the steering wheel. Marguerite says, we'll find a spot in the Bois de Boulogne where there aren't too many people. – Okay. Okay. We look for her car. Marguerite has forgotten where she parked it and I've forgotten what kind of car it is. I point out two or three before we land on the right one. She switches on the ignition and starts up. I watch her movements. She asks, have you brought your licence? – Yes. Do you think it's still valid? You don't get this kind of licence any more. Marguerite glances at it and says, I've got the same. – What kind of car is this? – A Peugeot 207 automatic. – Automatic! I don't know how to drive an automatic! – It's very easy. Much easier than a manual. There's nothing to do. – Oh dear. An automatic! Marguerite says, don't mention this to Odile, you promise, all right? I don't want a ticking-off from your daughter. – Not a word. She annoys me the way she's overprotective towards me. I don't need kid-glove treatment. We drive around in the wood in search of quiet spot. We end up finding a small path intersected by a white barrier that's five metres wide. Marguerite parks. She turns off the engine. We each get out to swap places. We laugh a little. I say, I don't know how to do anything any more, Marguerite. She says, you've got two pedals. The brake and the accelerator. You control them with one foot. Your left foot has nothing to do. Switch on the ignition. I switch on the ignition. The engine purrs. I turn to face Marguerite, encouraged at having switched on the ignition so easily. Well done, says Marguerite in her teacher's voice (she teaches Spanish). You were able to switch on the ignition because you were in P, for *parking*. Put your seat belt on. – Really? – Yes, yes. Marguerite leans over and secures the belt, which squashes me. I say, I feel like a prisoner. – You'll get used to it. Now you're going to put the selector into D for *drive*. Where's your right foot? – Nowhere. – Put it on the brake. – Why? – Because once you're in D all you have to do is ease off and the car will start up. – Really? – Yes. – Here we go. – Put it into D. I take a breath and put it into D. Nothing happens. Marguerite says, gently ease off with your foot. Go on, go on, take it off completely. I take it off completely. I'm extremely tense. The car moves. I say, it's moving! – Now put your foot on the accelerator. – Where is it? – Next to the brake, right next to it. I feel around with my foot, I find a pedal, I press down. The car comes to an abrupt halt, flinging us forward. The belt cuts into my chest. – What's happened? You put your foot back on the brake, says Marguerite. You jammed on the brakes. Now, put yourself into N. – What's N? – Neutral. As in standstill. – Ah, standstill! Yes, I see. – Let's start again. Brake. Drive. Give your left foot a rest, it doesn't need to do anything. – I don't know how to drive an automatic! – You soon will. That's it. Selector on D and relax. Bravo. Now move your foot slightly to the right to find the accelerator pedal and press down. I concentrate. The car moves. I hold my breath. The barrier is still a way off but I'm heading towards it without any degree of control. I panic. How do I brake? How do I stop? – Brake. – I stay in . . . in . . . what's it called? – Yes, you stay in D. And when the car stops, you go back into N. Into N, not R! R is for *reverse*. Don't use your left foot! You're pressing down on both pedals at the same time, Jeannette! We judder to a halt with an odd noise. I've broken out in a sweat. I say, I hope you're more patient with your students. – My students are a bit more on the ball. – You're the one who suggested I take up driving again. – You're languishing in your apartment, you need to be more independent. Switch the ignition on again. Go into P. What's your right foot doing? – I don't know. – Put it on the accelerator without pressing down. There you go. Into D. And off you go. Accelerate gently. My sister-in-law's instructions lodge in a remote part of my brain. I respond on autopilot. That sad lump is back in my throat. I try to get rid of it. We're moving. Where are you going? asks Marguerite. – I don't know. – Aim straight for the barrier. – Yes. – You can turn beforehand, on the grass. Go round the tree and come back the other way. She points to a place I can't see because I'm incapable of looking anywhere that's not straight ahead. Slow down, says Marguerite, slow down. She's making me feel stressed. I don't know how to slow down any more. My arms are welded to the steering wheel like two iron bars. Turn, turn, Jeannette! shouts Marguerite. I don't know where I am any more. Marguerite has grabbed the steering wheel. The barrier is two metres away. – Let go of the steering wheel, Jeannette! Take your foot off! She pulls on the brake and operates the gear selector. The car rears up, hits the white barrier and scrapes it. Then comes to a stop. Marguerite doesn't say a word. The tears that have welled up suddenly cloud my vision. Marguerite gets out. She walks around the back of the car before surveying the damage. She opens my door. She says, in a gentle voice (which is worse than anything), climb out, I'm going to reverse. She helps me take off my seat belt. She sits in my place and reverses briefly to extricate the 207 from the barrier. She gets out again. The front left is a bit smashed in, there's a broken headlight and it's scraped all along the right wing. I whisper, I'm sorry, forgive me. Marguerite says, well you've certainly given it a good seeing-to. – I'm sorry, Marguerite, I'll pay for all the repairs. She looks at me, Jeannette, you're not going to cry because of that? Oh, Jeannette, this is stupid, who cares about a little dent in a car? If you knew how many things I've crashed into in my life; one day, in front of the lycée, I nearly ran over a thirteen-year-old student. I say, forgive me, forgive me, I've ruined the whole day. Come on, in you get, says Marguerite, let's go and eat ice cream at Bagatelle. I've been wanting to go back to Bagatelle for months now. We return to our original seats. She starts up with no trouble. Marguerite reverses in the grass with a dexterity that aggrieves me. I understand people who like bad weather. It puts paid to ideas like visiting a flower garden. Cheer up, Jeannette, says Marguerite. That barrier was holding out its arms to us, it has to be said. To tell you the truth, I knew from the start you'd go into it. I smile in spite of myself. I say, don't ever tell Ernest. – Ha ha, I've got you! laughs Marguerite. I adore Marguerite. I wish I'd married her instead of her brother. I can hear the mobile phone going off in my bag.

Odile has set me up with a shrill ringtone because she thinks I'm deaf. Apart from Odile and Ernest, or my son-in-law Robert, nobody calls me on this phone. – Hello? – Mummy? – Yes? – Where are you? – In the Bois de Boulogne. – Right. Don't worry about it, but Daddy was having lunch with his friends from the Third Circle when he had a dizzy turn. The restaurant called an ambulance. They took him to the Pitié. – A turn . . . ? – Are you still with Marguerite? – Yes . . . – Have you found some pretty things? I say, what kind of a turn? Where are you, Odile? Odile's voice is muffled, a bit hollow. – At the Pitié-Salpêtrière. They're going to give him a coronary angiography to see if the bypasses are blocked. – If what? What are they going to do to him? – We're waiting for the tests. Don't worry about it. Tell me, did you try on the dress in Franck et Fils, Mummy?

Robert Toscano

Out of the blue, at the exit to the mortuary known as the Amphitheatre, on rue Bruant, at the moment when the boys are loading Ernest's coffin into the back of the hearse, my mother-in-law, Jeannette, overcome by some unfathomable terror, refuses to get into the funeral limousine. She's meant to be taking her place in there with Marguerite and the celebrant, who ranks himself master of ceremonies for the day, and I'm meant to follow them in the Volkswagen with Odile and my mother to the crematorium at Père-Lachaise. My mother-in-law, wearing uncustomary heels, retreats (and nearly falls) towards the wall, like an animal slated for the abattoir. With her back against the stone, beneath the blinding light, and frantically sweeping the air with her arms, she urges the Mercedes estate to move off without her, in full view of an alarmed Marguerite, who is already sitting in the back. Mummy, Mummy, says Odile, if you don't want to ride with Daddy, I'll go instead. You ride with Robert and Zozo. She takes her gently by the arm and leads her to the Volkswagen where my mother, slumped in the heat (summer has arrived all of a sudden), is waiting in the front seat. The celebrant rushes to open the back door but Jeannette stammers what turns out to be, I want to go in front. Odile whispers, Mummy, please, it's not important. – I wish to follow Ernest. It's my husband in there. Would you like me to stay with you, Mummy? Marguerite can accompany the coffin alone, says Odile, giving me a look that means, get your mother to change places. Clearly I don't react in the right way because Odile has already stuck her head into the car, Zozo, would you be kind enough to go in the back, Mummy isn't comfortable with the idea of riding in the Mercedes? My mother looks at me as if to say she thought she had seen it all. Without a word, and taking her time, she unfastens her seat belt, picks up her bag and extricates herself from the seat, emphasising the arthritic discomfort of such a manoeuvre. Thank you, Zozo, says Odile, that's very decent of you. Still without a word, and with the same heaviness of movement, fanning herself with one hand, my mother settles her body into the back. Jeannette sits in front without any sign of gratitude, her expression, in any event, no longer of this world. Odile climbs into the Mercedes with her aunt and the celebrant. I take the wheel to follow them to Père-Lachaise. After a pause, Jeannette says, her face intent on the windscreen and, beyond it, the black boot of the Mercedes, was your husband cremated, Zozo? My father is buried at the cemetery in Bagneux, I inform her. Jeannette seems to ponder this piece of information before turning around to ask, and will you have yourself put with him? Good question, says my mother. If it were just down to me, not on my life. I hate Bagneux. Nobody ever comes to see you there. It's the sticks. Ahead of us, the Mercedes is going at an exasperatingly slow pace. Is this part of the ritual? We stop at a red light. A hazy silence descends. I'm hot. My tie is too tight. The suit I'm wearing is too thick. Jeannette is searching for something in her bag. I can't abide the semi-muffled clinking and the sound of rubbed leather produced by such rummaging. Made worse by the fact that she sighs and I can't abide people who sigh. What are you looking for, Jeannette? I say after a while. – The page from *Le Monde*, I haven't even had time to read it. I thrust my right hand into her bag and help her to pull out the article, which is folded and crumpled. – Can you read it out? Jeannette puts on her glasses and recites in a doleful voice, 'Death of Ernest Blot. A banker as influential as he was secret. Born in 1939, Ernest Blot passed away during the night of 23 June, at the age of seventy-three. With him dies one of those figures of the French investment banking elite, who came from the public service, and whose expertise was matched only by his discretion. After graduating top of his year from ENA in 1965' – top, you see, I'd forgotten about that – 'he joined the Inspectorate-General of Finances. He went on to serve on several ministerial staffs between 1969 and 1978, as well as consulting in' . . . blah, blah, we know all that . . . 'In 1979, he joined the Wurmster Bank, founded in the aftermath of the First World War, but at the time rather outdated, becoming its chief financial officer and then, in 1985, CEO. He transformed it, little by little, into one of France's premier financial institutions, on a par with Lazard Frères, Rothschild' . . . blah, blah . . . 'He wrote a biography of Achille Fould, Minister of Finance for the 2nd Republic (éditions Perrin, 1997). Ernest Blot was a Grand Officer of the National Order of Merit and a Commander of the Legion of Honour' . . . Not a word about his wife. Is that normal? I never opened the Achille Fould. It sold three copies. The prospect of reading it made me feel queasy. My mother says, we're stifling in this car, can you turn up the air con, darling? No air con! shrieks Jeannette, no air con, it gets right inside my skull. I glance in the rear-view mirror. My mother has rearranged herself so as not to contradict the widow of the day. She has simply tilted her head back and opened her mouth like a carp. From out of her bag Jeannette produces a pocket electric fan with transparent blades. – Here you go, Zozo, this will cool you down. She turns it on. It sounds like a deranged wasp. She completes two circles around her own face then offers it to my mother. Don't need it, gasps my mother. – Try it, Zozo, really. – No thanks. – Take it, Mum, you're hot. – I'm perfectly fine, leave me alone. Jeannette quickly runs the fan over one side of her neck then the other. My mother says, in a hollow

183

voice, just behind my ear, I still haven't forgiven your father for not selling that wretched plot. When I die, Robert, move us. Bury us in the city. Paulette told me there are still some plots left in the Jewish enclosure at Montparnasse. The Mercedes turns left, performing a sort of majestic circle, briefly revealing Odile and Marguerite in silent profile. Jeannette says, I don't feel anything at all. She seems lost. Arms by her sides, handbag on her knees, the buzzing fan in a lifeless hand. I sense that I need to respond in some way, to make a remark, but nothing comes to me. Ernest held an important place in my life. He took an interest in my work (I used to read some of my articles to him before sending them to the newspaper), he would fire questions at me, he debated with me in the way I would have liked my own father to have done (my father was kindly and affectionate, but he didn't know how to be the father of a grown man). Ernest and I would call each other almost every morning to sort out Syria or Iran, to criticise the naivety of the West or the European sense of entitlement. That was his hobby horse. The fact that we had now taken to lecturing others after a thousand years of massacres. I have lost a friend who had a view of life. Which is rare.

People don't have a view of life. They just have opinions. Talking to Ernest always made you feel less alone. I know he can't have been much fun for Jeannette on a daily basis. One morning (he was leaving for a conference on currency), she threw a cup of coffee in his face. – You are a despicable person, you have ruined my life as a woman. As he wiped his jacket Ernest had said, your life as a woman? What is a life as a woman? When I met Odile, he said to me, she's bloody annoying, I'm warning you, I'm grateful to you for taking her off my hands. And later on, don't worry, young man, the first marriage is always hard. I had asked him, were you married many times? – No, and that's precisely my point. My mother is talking in the back. I take a moment to return to my senses and grasp the meaning of her words. She says, it is afterwards that one feels something. When all the fuss of death is over. When the fuss is over, the only thing I'll feel is bitterness, says Jeannette. That's overstating it, I say. She shakes her head, was he a good husband, your one, Zozo? Uhhh . . . , says my mother. – What d'you mean, Mum? You were happy with Dad, weren't you? – I wasn't unhappy. No. But a good husband doesn't roam the streets, you know. We head up avenue Gambetta in silence. The trees cast a quivering shadow. Jeannette is rummaging in her bag again. Somebody toots a horn to my left. I'm about to launch into a diatribe when I spot, level with us, the smiling faces (burial-style) of the Hutners. Lionel is at the wheel, Pascaline is leaning out of the window so as to give Jeannette a wave. I glance briefly behind me. Before accelerating, I have enough time to notice their son Jacob, sitting in the back, upright and intense-looking, with a sort of Indian scarf wrapped round his neck. Did you invite the Hutners? says Jeannette as if this is too much for her. – We invited our close friends. The Hutners were very fond of Ernest. – For the love of God, it'll kill me having to greet all those people. It'll kill me. All this lip service. For a shitty cremation with a bloody mortician who gets on my nerves. She pulls down the front sun visor to check her face in the mirror. As she's putting on some lipstick, she says, do you know who I've invited? Raoul Barnèche. – Who's that? – There's something none of you know about, not even Odile, nobody will write it up in any newspaper, it's something I endured all alone. When he recovered from his bypasses, in 2002, Ernest started brooding. Brooding, morning and night, slumped in his chair under the painting of the unicorn, fussing over the food on his plate, refusing any kind of rehabilitation. He thought it was all over. Albert, his driver, had the idea of introducing him to his brother who's a champion card player. This man, Raoul Barnèche, handsome, you'll see, a sort of Robert Mitchum, came nearly every day to play gin rummy with him. They played for money. Larger and larger sums. It brought Ernest back to life. I had to put a stop to it before he was completely fleeced. But it saved him. We enter the cemetery, on the side of the funeral parlour, rue des Rondeaux. The Mercedes comes to a halt in front of the columbarium. There are people on the steps and between the columns. I share Jeannette's anxiety. Odile and Marguerite are already outside. A man in black points to the car park on the left. I say to the women, would you like to get out? But neither of them wants to get out and I understand. I park. We flank the building. Odile comes to greet her mother. She says, there are more than a hundred people, the doors to the room are still closed. I can see Paola Suares, the Condamines, the Hutners, Marguerite's children, and Doctor Ayoun to whose consulting room I accompanied Ernest on several occasions. I spot Jean Ehrenfried climbing the steps one by one, propped up by Darius Ardashir, who is carrying his crutch for him. Set back, near to a bush, I recognise Albert, my father-in-law's driver. He is with another man in mafia-style glasses at whom Jeannette smiles. They come over to us. Albert puts his arms around my mother-in-law. When he lets go his eyes are moist and his face seems to have shrunk. He says, twenty-seven years. Jeannette repeats the figure. I wonder whether Jeannette has any idea what he must have seen and hidden from her in the course of those twenty-seven years. She turns towards the dark man in the corduroy jacket and takes his hand, it's so kind of you to have come, Raoul. The man removes his glasses and says, it has affected me greatly. Jeannette doesn't let go of his hand. She moves it jerkily. He plays along with this, a bit embarrassed. She says, Raoul Barnèche. He used to play gin rummy with Ernest. She's right, he does look a bit like Robert Mitchum. A dimple on his chin, puffy eyes and rebellious hair. Jeannette is all flushed. He smiles. In the courtyard outside the crematorium, under a uniformly blue sky, with family, friends and officials waiting for her, my mother-in-law is clinging to a man I have never heard of before. I can sense movement around us. The doors open between the columns.

I'm looking for my mother who has disappeared. I spot her with the Hutners at the bottom of the steps. Odile joins us there. She kisses Jacob warmly, I haven't seen you in so long, have you grown again? In a voice that is slow and sustained, with a pronounced Québécois accent, Jacob says, Odile, you know that I also lost my father, of course it was difficult but I've made space for him inside my heart. He folds his hands on his chest and adds, I know he's here with me. Odile glances at me in alarm. I blink reassuringly at her. I mouth, I'll explain later. I take hold of Lionel's arm as his face is now mummified, and I load up my mother on the other side. She is about to pass comment as we climb the stone staircase but I encourage her to refrain by squeezing her. The room fills up in silence. I seat my mother and the Hutners and head off to play my role as host among the rows. I greet the family members, Ernest's cousins from Brittany, André Taneux, a fellow student of Ernest's at ENA, who was the first President of the Court of Auditors, the boss of my press group (Odile approves of his ridiculous three-day beard), some people I don't recognise, the chief of staff to the Minister of Finance, the Director of the Inspectorate-General of Finances, some former colleagues from the Inspectorate who spontaneously shake my hand. Darius Ardashir introduces me to the Chairman of the Board of Directors of the Third Circle. I run into Odile again among the staff of the Wurmster Bank. She's wearing her Maître Toscano hairdo. She appears unfazed. She whispers into my ear, Jacob . . . ?! I don't have time to answer because the master of ceremonies urges us to take our seats in the front row along with Marguerite, her children and Jeannette. The congregation stands. Ernest's coffin is brought into the aisle. The bearers lay it down on trestles at the base of the steps leading to the catafalque. The celebrant has moved to the lectern. Behind him, at the top of the double flight of stairs, surrounding the raised platform, is a painted city that is half-Jerusalem, half-Babel, scattered with biblical poplars, bathed in a blue twilight that is kitsch of the highest order. The celebrant encourages a few moments of silence. I picture Ernest lying in the close-fitting Lanvin suit from the sixties which Jeannette has chosen. Me too, I think to myself, one day I'll be stifled in that box of death, all alone. And Odile as well. And the children. And everybody here, whatever their rank, whether they're old or not, whether they're happy or not, busily keeping their place among the living. All utterly alone. Ernest wore that suit for years. Even when it had long since gone out of fashion, even when his paunch should have proscribed wearing the slim-fit, double-breasted jacket. On his way back from Brussels one day, driving way over the speed limit, Ernest had eaten a packet of barbecue-flavoured crisps, a chicken sandwich and a bar of nougat. Less than five minutes later, he had turned into a giant toad, asphyxiated by the Lanvin suit and the safety belt. He drove a Peugeot convertible, and as he arrived into Paris a pigeon shat on him. I'm looking for the Hutners. They've moved to the end of the row just in front of the Condamines. Jacob is on the outside. Humble and reserved, I note, like somebody who doesn't want to attract any attention. André Taneux has replaced the master of ceremonies behind the lectern. Big backcombed hair dyed a drastic brown (faintly purple under the watery light from the stained-glass windows). He was the one who insisted on saying a few words despite the reluctance of Odile and Jeannette. He unfolds his piece of paper slowly and adjusts the microphone to little effect. – An imposing figure has suddenly departed, leaving in his wake a waft of Gauloises and aristocracy.

Ernest Blot has left us. If I am playing my part today and making my voice heard, Jeannette, thank you, I am doing so because in Ernest we are not merely losing somebody dear to us. We are losing a happy period of our history. In France, in the aftermath of the war, faced with the rubble and the debris, there rose up one of those unexpected parties, capable of uniting people from all walks of life and of all convictions, believers and atheists, from the right and the left: the party of modernisation. With the same hand, it was necessary to rebuild both the State and the business infrastructure, to resolve the deficit and to place it at the service of growth. Our friend Ernest Blot was one of the emblematic figures of this party. ENA, the Inspectorate-General of Finances, several ministerial staffs, the investment banking elite: a continuous lifeline in an era which, alas, no longer exists, when the graduates of ENA were not technocrats but builders, when the State didn't mean conservatism but progress, when banking didn't mean the crazy money of a globalised casino but the relentless financing of channels of productivity. An era when men with values didn't make careers or fortunes but served their country, in both public and private sectors, being neither venal nor vain. However great my sadness at losing Ernest, I comfort myself with the thought that this noble spirit has taken his leave of a world which no longer resembles him. Rest in peace, my friend, far from an era that is not worthy of you. And now hurry off to the hair colourist's, old pal, I whisper to Odile. Taneux folds his piece of paper with pursed lips and returns to his seat. The celebrant waits for his steps to fade on the marble. He leaves a pause and then says, Monsieur Jean Ehrenfried, director, former CEO of Safranz-Ulm Electric. Darius Ardashir is bending over Jean to help him stand up and lean on his crutch. Jean limps gingerly towards the lectern. He is thin and pale, dressed in a beige-checked suit and a tie with yellow polka dots. He puts his free hand on the ledge to steady himself. The wood creaks and reverberates. Jean looks at the coffin, and then straight ahead towards the back of the room. He takes out neither paper nor glasses. – Ernest . . . you used to say to me, what will I say about you at your funeral? And I used to reply, you will sing the praises of a stateless old Jew, try to be deep for once. I was older than you, and more sick, we hadn't foreseen the reverse situation . . . We would call each other regularly. The phrase that sticks in my head is *where are you?* Where are you? We were often here and there because of work but you had Plou-Gouzan L'Ic, your house near Saint-Brieuc. You had your house and your apple trees, in a small valley. When I used to say, where are you, and you replied, at Plou-Gouzan L'Ic, I was jealous of you. You really were somewhere. You had forty apple trees. Every year you made twenty litres of revolting cider which I ended up by liking . . . He breaks off. He sways and holds onto the lectern. The celebrant is on the verge of stepping in but Jean prevents him. – A harsh, unfermented cider, to use your own description, in plastic detergent bottles, a far cry from the corked and sparkling ciders of the bourgeoisie. It was your cider. It came from your apples, from your land . . . Where are you now? Where are you? I know that your body is in this two-metre coffin. But what about you, where are you? Not long ago, in my doctor's waiting room, a female patient said this: even life, beyond a certain point, is an idiotic value. It is true that at the end of the race one alternates between the temptation to oppose death vigorously (I recently purchased an exercise bicycle) and the desire to let oneself slip towards I don't know what dark place . . . Are you waiting for me somewhere, Ernest?

194

Where? That is perhaps not the final word. It is barely audible and might equally be the first syllable of an abandoned sentence. Jean falls quiet. He has turned almost fully round to face the coffin. In several tiny stages, careful not to let the deficient body be seen. His lips half open and then close again, like the beak of a famished bird. His right arm holds his stick so firmly that it rocks. He stays for some time in this fragile position, whispering, one might say, in the ear of the dead. Then he looks across the room in the direction of Darius, who immediately comes to help him back to his place. I squeeze Odile's hand and I see that she is crying. The celebrant has taken the microphone back and announces the committal of the coffin of Ernest Blot for cremation, in accordance, he says, with the wishes he had himself expressed. The bearers lift the coffin again. The congregation stands. The bearers climb the steps in silence as far as the catafalque, which seems absurdly high and far. A mechanism starts up. Ernest disappears.

Odile Toscano

The final year of her life, your grandmother rather lost her head, says Marguerite. She kept wanting to go and pick up her children from the village. I would say, Mother, you don't have small children any more. I do, I do, and I need to bring them home. We would set off to collect her children from le Petit-Quevilly. It was a good excuse to make her walk. It was funny going to collect Ernest and myself from sixty years earlier. We've passed Rennes. Marguerite has the window seat, next to Robert. Since the start of our journey, hers is pretty much the only voice we've been hearing. She's directing it all at me, in sporadic bursts (the other two having withdrawn into a fug of privacy), as she digs up various past seasons of the dead. We're in one of those new compartments that is open onto the corridor. Mummy is sitting opposite Marguerite. She has jammed the Go Sport bag between us. She didn't want to put it up in the luggage rack. Robert has been in a sulk ever since he found out that we need to change at Guingamp. It was my secretary's mistake. She booked return tickets from Paris to Guernonzé with a change on the outbound journey. When he realised this, at Gare Montparnasse, Robert accused us of always wanting to complicate everything when it would have been so easy to go by car. He strode ahead of us onto the platform, livid, carrying the striped black-and-pink Go Sport bag containing the urn. I can't begin to understand the choice of bag. Nor can Marguerite. She whispered in my ear, why has your mother put Ernest in that? Didn't they have a more presentable travel bag? Through the window warehouses and scattered dreary industrial estates flash past. Further off, housing estates and fields of ploughed earth. I can't make my seat comfortable. It keeps thrusting me forward, or that's how it feels. Robert asks me what I'm trying to do. I'm preventing him reading, a biography of Hannibal. On the cover is an epigraph from Juvenal: 'Great

Hannibal within the balance lay, / And tell how many pounds his ashes weigh.' My mother has shut her eyes. Hands on lap, she lets herself be rocked by the movement of the train. Her skirt rides up too high over her blouse, which is unduly tucked in. It's been a long time since I've taken a proper look at her. A woman nobody pays any attention to, plump and tired. At Cabourg, when I was little, she used to walk on the promenade in a chiffon dress that was nipped in at the waist. The pale fabric would float, and she would swing her cloth bag in the wind. The train passes through Lamballe without stopping. We have time to spot the car park, the doctor's red house (Marguerite almost shouts this information at us), the station buildings, the fortified church. Every outline made hazy by a perfidious mist. I think of Daddy crossing his childhood town for the last time, ground up in a sports bag. I feel like seeing Rémi. I feel like having some fun. How about trying out those nipple clamps Paola mentioned? Poor Paola. Dragged around by Luc (I wonder if Robert knows). If I were a generous friend, I'd introduce her to Rémi Grobe. They'd like each other. But I want to keep Rémi for myself. Rémi rescues me from Robert, from time, and from the general gloom. Last night, Robert and I remained in the dark for a long time without talking. At one point I said, who is Lionel for Jacob these days? I sensed that Robert was pondering this and that he didn't know. The train stops at Saint-Brieuc. A long line of white houses, all identical. A truck from the cooperative Starlette de Plouaret-Bretagne has run aground, set back from the platform. The poor Hutners. Still, who else could it happen to? The train moves off again. Marguerite says, the next stop is Guingamp. When we used to come to Plou-Gouzan L'Ic, we would get off at Saint-Brieuc. I've never been any further. Daddy never took me any further than Plou-Gouzan L'Ic, the hole where he had bought the mouldy house which he adored and which Mummy and I hated. It was Luc who supplied the handcuffs and the nipple clamps, according to Paola. Rémi doesn't come up with ideas like that. I can't go buying them in person. Over the Internet? Where would I get the package delivered to? Guingamp, calls out Marguerite. We rush to stand up as if the train was only stopping for five and a half seconds. Robert grabs the Go Sport bag. Marguerite and Mummy throw themselves at the doors. Change at Guingamp. A sign attached to a glass shelter indicates Brest. Marguerite says, we stay here. A damp gust slides down my neck. I say, it's cold. Marguerite isn't having any of it. She doesn't want anybody criticising Brittany. She is wearing a purple trouser suit that's done up all the way to the neck. A silk scarf covers her shoulders. She has made an effort with her appearance as if for a lovers' tryst. In the middle of the platform, in a glass cage, people are lined up along a single bench. Pasty travellers, wedged together in front of a mound of bags. I say, Mummy, would you like to sit down? – In there? Absolutely not. She puts on her overcoat. Robert helps her. She's wearing flat shoes for the occasion. She glances in the direction of the old-fashioned clock, towards the sky, and at the slow-moving clouds. She says, do you know what I'm thinking of? My little Austrian pine. I'd like to see it show its face today. Mummy had planted an Austrian pine among the apple trees at Plou-Gouzan L'Ic. Daddy had said, your mother thinks she's everlasting. She bought a fifteen-centimetre tree because it's cheaper; she thinks she'll still be here to walk around it with Simon's great-grandson. Robert says, with a bit of luck it should reach your shoulders, Jeannette, provided nobody's pulled it out with the weeds. We laugh. I can almost hear Daddy laughing in the bag. My mother ends up saying, perhaps it was too cramped for it to grow in the middle of the apple trees. Robert strolls towards the end of the platform. The back of his jacket is crumpled. He walks along by the tracks, still clutching the reason for our trip, swaying from foot to foot, in search of who knows what view from the empty platform. The train we catch from Guingamp to Guernonze makes the sound of a railway from a bygone era. The windows are dirty. We pass some huts, some grain silos, then the view is blocked by the guardrail and the undergrowth. Nobody says much. Robert has put Hannibal away (a few days ago, he commented, what a marvellous human being), and he's busy on his BlackBerry. Guernonze. The sky has cleared. We emerge from the station into a car park, surrounded by white buildings with grey roofs. On the other side of the square, an Ibis Hotel. Marguerite says, it was nothing like this before. Cars are parked in the middle of a riot of bollards, street lamps and saplings imprisoned by wooden posts. In the old days, none of this was here, says Marguerite. Nor was the Ibis, it's very recent all this. She takes Mummy's arm. We cross the roundabout. We're walking along a narrow pavement lined with deserted houses all shuttered up. The road curves. The cars heading in both directions brush against us. Here's the bridge, says Marguerite. – The bridge? – The bridge over the Braïve. I feel thwarted that it should be this close to the station. I wasn't expecting our procession to be so brief. Marguerite points to an apartment block on the other side and says, our grandparents' house was just behind that. It's half demolished. It's a dry cleaner's these days. Do you want to see it? – There's no point. – Where that apartment block is, there was a garden with a wash house that gave on to the Braïve. We used to play there. Did you spend all your holidays at Guernonze? I say. – Summers. And Easters. But Easter was depressing. The bridge is framed by a black iron guardrail. There are flower boxes hanging off it. No let-up in the cars going past. In the distance, a hill that's largely been developed prompts Marguerite to say, it used to be just greenery up there. Is this where we're throwing the ashes? asks Mummy. If that's what you want, says Marguerite. I don't want anything at all, says Mummy. – This is where we scattered our father's ashes. – Why not on the other side? It's prettier. Because the current flows this way, says Robert. An estate agent's, that must be very recent, says Marguerite pointing at the street that runs parallel to the opposite bank. Marguerite, please, stop telling us which things did or didn't exist, nobody cares, nobody's interested, says my mother. Marguerite pulls a sour face. No words of appeasement come to mind because I agree more. Robert has opened the Go Sport bag. He takes out the metal urn. My mother looks all around, it's ghastly doing this in broad daylight, in the middle of the traffic. – We don't have a choice, Mummy. – It doesn't feel at all special. Robert asks, who's going to do it? You, Robert, you, says Mummy. Why not Odile? says Marguerite – Robert will do a better job. Robert holds out the urn to me. I won't touch it. Ever since it was given back to us at the crematorium, I can't bring myself to hold that urn. I say, she's right, do it. Robert opens the first lid which he hands me. I chuck it into the bag. He unscrews the second lid without removing it. He passes his arm over the railing. The women huddle together like two frightened birds. Robert takes off the second lid and tips the urn upside down. Grey sawdust escapes, dispersing in the air and falling back down onto the Braive. Robert hugs me. We watch the calm river, streaked with little waves, the trees that border it stretched out like black marks. Behind us, the cars sound noisier and noisier as they go past. Marguerite picks a white flower from one of the flower boxes and throws it. The flower is too light. It flies off towards the left and scarcely lands on the water before catching in a pile of stones. On the other side of a footbridge, some children are getting ready for a canoeing trip. What shall we do with the urn? asks Mummy. We'll throw it away, says Robert, who has put it back in the bag. – Where? – In a bin. There's one by the wall over there. I suggest we head back to the station. Let me buy you all a drink while we're waiting for the train. We leave the bridge. I stare at the water, the line of yellow buoys. I take my leave of Daddy. I blow a little kiss. When he reaches the corner, Robert tries to stuff the Go Sport bag into the bin. – What are you doing, Robert? Why are you throwing the bag away? – It's a disgusting bag. You're not going to do anything with it, Jeannette. – Yes I am. It's useful for carrying things around. Don't throw it away. Mummy, I intervene, this bag held Daddy's ashes, it has served its purpose. That's completely ridiculous, says my mother, this bag has carried a vase, full stop. Robert, please, take that crappy urn, throw it away and give me back the bag. – That bag is worth ten euros, Mummy! – I want the bag back! – Why? – Because! I'm already fool enough to have traipsed out here, now I'd like to decide a few things for myself. Your father is in his river, everything's in order, and I'm going back to Paris with my bag. Give me that bag, Robert. Robert has emptied the bag and is holding it out to my mother. I grab it out of his hands, Mummy, please, this is grotesque. She snatches the handle, moaning, it's my bag, Odile! I shout, this shitty bag is staying in Guernonze! I cram it into the bin. We hear a savage, heart-rending sob. Marguerite has raised her hands and lifted her face to the sky like a *pietà*. I begin to cry myself. Now look what you've done, congratulations, says Mummy. Robert tries to calm her and steer her away from the bin. She puts up a bit of a fight, then, hanging onto his arm, concedes to walk back up the narrow pavement, staggering almost, her body hugging the stone wall. I watch them walking, him with his hair that's too long, his crumpled jacket, Hannibal poking out of his pocket, her with those flat heels, her skirt showing below her overcoat, and it occurs to me that Robert is the more bereft of the two. Marguerite blows her nose. She is one of those women who always has a cotton handkerchief up her sleeve. I give her a kiss. Her warm fingers wrap around the palm of my hand and squeeze it. We walk back along the pavement, a few metres behind Mummy and Robert. At the end of the street, in front of the station car park, Marguerite stops opposite a low house with openings framed by red brick. She says, Ernest appeared in *The Battle of the Rails* on this spot. – Here? – Yes. Our grandparents told me about it, I wasn't born. He was there, among the extras, in front of a bistro that no longer exists. They were filming a hay cart. Ernest was just behind it, he thought we'd be able to see his legs at least. We catch up with Robert and my mother at the crossroads. He saw the film five or six times. Even as an old man, and you're witness to this, Jeannette, he would watch it when it came on telly in the hope of seeing his seven-year-old legs.

Jean Ehrenfried

A few years ago, Ernest, you and I, remember, before you sold Plou-Gouzan L'Ic, we went fishing. You had bought some angling tackle which you had never used and we set off to fish for trout, or carp, or who knows what freshwater fish, in a river close to your house. On the footpath, we felt absurdly happy. I had never fished, you neither, apart from a few shellfish by the seaside. After half an hour, perhaps less, we got a bite. You started tugging, overjoyed (I think I even helped you), and there wriggling at the end of the line we saw a small frightened fish. Which, in turn, made us feel frightened, Ernest, and you said to me, what shall we do? I called out, let it go, let it go! You succeeded in freeing it and releasing it back into the water. We packed up immediately after that. On the way back, not a word, we both felt fairly overwhelmed. All of a sudden you stopped and you said to me: two titans.

Translator's Acknowledgements

The translator wishes to thank Yasmina Reza and Michal Shavit for their patience and encouragement; Sam Gordon for his brilliantly insightful close reading and suggestions, as well as his diligent checking; Anneesa Higgins for 'purveyor of fine cheeses' in the first Robert Toscano chapter; Christopher Adams for kindly making sense of the bridge terms in the Raoul Barnèche chapter; Ros Schwartz and Géraldine D'Amico, translation fairy godmothers; also, Judy and Stephen Kane, and Emma Nightingale, for their generous hospitality. And finally, Simon Ardizzone, for everything.